House on Highland Road

Melissa Peters

To my dad,
because he asked for this dedication.
(I told you I'd put this in here.)

And to everyone who believed in me.

Chapter One

"*Seriously? You're going to waste your life like this? Pretending to be me?*"

My dead best friend, Riley, sits on the counter beside the milk steamer, swinging her legs. The cupboard beneath her rattles.

"*You're better than this, Lanie.*"

I ignore her. She's not really there—just a figment of my imagination. I scrub at an invisible spot with my bar cloth. Maybe if I continue to ignore her, she'll go away. The bell above the door jingles—bright and cheery. I paste on a smile and turn, but it's just a couple leaving the coffee shop.

"Have a nice day," I call after them.

I turn around and nearly trip over Riley. She's standing right in front of me. She looks exactly the same as the last day I saw her, with short, spiky black hair, dark eye makeup, and ears lined with piercings. She's always been the complete opposite of me. Even now, while trying to be her—live the life she might have chosen—I wear my golden-brown hair long and straight and keep my face free of everything but coverup and lip balm. My only piercings are my earlobes. Even my silvery blue eyes look innocent, unlike Riley's, which were always tinted with mischief or rebellion. Riley hadn't had a lot of money, but the little she'd had, she devoted to making herself look edgy and fringe. Her foster parents had hated it, but I loved it. Underneath the outward rebellion, she had been the sweetest, most caring person I'd known.

But that was last year. She'd died the day before her seventeenth birthday. It still haunts me, wondering if I could have said or done something to save her. Tears prick at my eyes.

The door chimes again. I scrub a hand over my face to keep the tears back. A woman in a sundress and floppy hat enters, as though it's the height of summer and not September, tourist season almost gone. Admittedly, the days are still hot, but the nights are getting cold. In a couple weeks, it'll be too cold to stay in Salvation Hills, living in my car. My seasonal job here at the café will be over. I'll have to come up with a new plan soon. Maybe I'll head south and live the tourist life myself. If only I could afford it.

The woman in the sundress eyes the menu board. It's littered with regular coffee drinks and silly ones named after places around town, like the Sweetgrass Cove Cappuccino. It doesn't actually have sweetgrass in it. It's made with lemongrass, but people love it.

"I'll have a Salvation Hills Fog. Iced, please."

As I key in her order, I force a smile, ignoring the phantom pressing in against my shoulder. Riley's breath ghosts against my neck. She's not real, but still, my skin pebbles under the chill. It's got to be the air conditioning. Ghosts don't breathe.

The Salvation Hills Fog is a London Fog mixed with salted caramel syrup instead of vanilla. I've become a pro at mixing it up this summer. When it's ready, I take it out to the woman in the sundress. She takes it from me and presses a dollar into my hand before leaving. Tourists are hit or miss on tipping. A dollar tip for a seven-dollar drink isn't that bad, I guess. It won't buy enough gas to fill my tank, though.

As I pass the window, I take a moment to stare out. Salvation Hills is one of those towns that just feels historical. Here on Main Street, there are boardwalks instead of sidewalks. They continue down past the hotels and onto the beach, so you can walk without your shoes filling with sand. The rest of the town has regular concrete sidewalks, or none at all, depending on which area you're in and when it was built. The modernized historical buildings where the tourists lurk are all kept really nice. They're painted each year to keep them from looking weathered after the brutal seaside winters. The further you go into town, the rougher the buildings look. Most homeowners just can't afford to paint every year.

There's a flyer posted on the wooden lamp post outside the shop, advertising a "spooky ghost tour". It might be the end of one tourist season, but it's never too soon to entice them back for the next. I have to admit, Salvation Hills looks like a place that might house spirits. It's got the history. If only I believed in ghosts.

I look around for the figment of my imagination, but she's gone now. I don't know when she disappeared. My mind's strange like that. Sighing, I turn back to the café. I've got to get ready to close.

"Hey, Riley?" Claire calls out from the back. It takes me a moment to realize that she's talking to me. I've been living under Riley's name since I left home. It feels better than my own, safer since I ran away in the middle of the night last year, shortly after Riley's death. I'd just hit a point where I couldn't take it anymore. I'd felt like I was going to implode if I didn't do something. So I'd left. It's not like anyone cared. And now I don't even know if my parents are looking for me. But it doesn't matter.

I take a breath before slipping into the kitchen at the back of the shop. Claire's spraying dishes down in the dish pit.

"Yeah?"

"Can you take out the trash? I'll put through this load of dishes."

A few minutes later, I'm tossing two enormous black trash bags into the bin behind the building, scrunching my nose at the reek of rotting coffee that wafts out of it. That done, I turn and look down the alley. From this vantage point, on one of the many rolling hills that Salvation Hills sits on, I have a clear view of the water. Not open ocean, but the delta where the brown-green water of the Broad River meets the navy water of the Atlantic. Sails dot the surface as the boats make their way to shore, coming home.

I wonder if I'll ever go home. But if the real Riley Miller couldn't handle it, there's no chance I could. I'm better off here, even without long-term plans. At least here there's no criticism. No constant judgement from my parents on how I should be better.

No sidelong glances and snide comments from my peers. I can be myself, even if I don't have an actual bed or a closet full of clothes. It's almost relaxing, though I worry about my future sometimes, about what I'll become if I stay here forever.

There's a knock on the open back door of the shop. My boss, Heather McIntyre, stands in the doorway, halfway into the alley. The wind whips her red curls about her face. "Can I interrupt?"

"Sorry," I say, wiping my hands on my apron and hurrying towards the door. "I was taking out the trash."

"You're not in trouble, Riley. It's okay to take in the view."

She hands me an envelope. Bold pen strokes scrawled across the front read *Riley Miller*.

"Payday!" she says.

"Thanks." I rip open the end and shake out the slip of paper. This one has my legal name, *Lanie Gilbert*, typed across the front. The only person in all of Salvation Hills who knows my legal name is Heather. I cringe seeing it in writing, then fold up the paycheque and shove it in my pocket. I'll deposit it after work. Heather is looking at me, concern radiating from her brown eyes.

"Are you okay, Riley?"

"Of course," I blurt out. I don't like this empathetic tone. It brings repressed tears to the forefront. Where's she going with this?

Heather frowns at my immediate response. "I know you're independent, but you're still young. Living alone... and after that woman went missing, too? I worry about you, Riley. I thought I saw your car parked in the Walmart parking lot late last night.

It was nearly two in the morning. Are you sure you're all right? You're not living in your car, are you? You have a place to stay?"

I bristle at her tone. I have a place to sleep. That's more than some people have. Sure, it has four wheels and six windows. It might not be a house, and most people would consider me homeless for it. But it's my home. Of course, it doesn't help that a Salvation Hills resident went missing last week. If Heather finds out, she'll worry about me. Maybe feel obligated to offer me a bed or tell the police and they'll start doing checks on me, or worse, report my whereabouts to my parents. Then I'll really have to leave Salvation Hills if I want to lie low. So I lie to Heather. "No, I'm not living out of my car. I really wanted some chocolate so I made a late-night trip."

It's not entirely a lie. I had bought chocolate at Walmart, just not late at night.

She nods, but gives me a disbelieving look. "Walmart is better than the gas station at that hour, I suppose."

"Thanks for worrying about me." I move towards the door and she steps back, letting me enter the café before her.

"Riley." She touches my arm as I pass her. Her voice is low, kind. I swallow back a rush of tears, her soft touch jarring. "I get it. If you need anything, just ask. You can't do everything on your own, you know what I mean?"

I nod briskly. It's easier said than done. If she could give me a job over the winter, that'd be great. Then I might be able to make it on my own here. I've saved enough for a cheap apartment if I can find one, but everyone complains how much Salvation Hills shuts down in the winter, how those months are tight for everyone. I can't ask her to keep me on.

The door jingles. Three customers walk in. Two guys and a girl, all around my age, maybe a little older. One of the guys has copper hair and hazel eyes. A spattering of freckles dots his pale skin. The other is your typical tall, dark and handsome: olive skin, raven hair, and pensive eyes. He seems reserved and shrewd. His eyes scan the coffee shop before he dismisses it. The woman has golden-brown skin, with hair dyed a silvery shade of amethyst. Her makeup is perfect. She's too beautiful. I'm instantly intimidated by her. I can't imagine how her girl friends must feel around her.

Claire greets them brightly. "Welcome to The Roasted Bean!"

They jostle each other like close friends as they stare at the menu board.

"I better go help Claire," I tell Heather, excusing myself from our conversation. I wash my hands, then make the drinks they've ordered, placing them on a tray to take out to the rectangular table they're sitting at. They're our only customers, aside from two others who've been nursing their drinks for an hour. By this time of day, late afternoon, most people are moving on to beverages of a stronger variety. Their conversation is low, but the murmur of it fills the small shop. I balance the tray carefully in front of me as I approach.

"Hello there," the redhead says. I can tell he's older than my eighteen years, but not by much. Up close, his eyes are more green than brown. He smiles readily. I can't tell if he's flirting or just being friendly. I blink rapidly, heat spreading up my neck, and set the tray down before I drop it.

"Hi." I distribute their drinks and pick up the tray, holding it like a shield in front of me. "Can I get you anything else?"

"Can I get your number?" the redhead asks, leaning towards me. He immediately flinches and glares at his dark-haired companion. "What was that for?"

"Try concentrating on the case for once, instead of every pretty girl that walks by." His friend turns to me. "No offense. I'm sure my friend would appreciate your number if you wanted to give it to him."

I let out a nervous laugh, backing away from the table. "That's okay."

My face burns as I rush into the kitchen to escape my embarrassment.

"What was that?" Claire pokes me in the ribs as I walk by. She winks, so I know she's not being malicious. "A little awkward, huh?"

"A little? What's wrong with me?"

She leans against a counter and taps her chin. "He's cute. You just need some practise flirting. It'll be easy in no time. Spend some time with me. I'll give you tips. I've got decades of experience."

"And yet, you're still single," I tease, her words easing some of my embarrassment.

She shoots me a wry look, then grins. "I'm single for a reason. Doesn't mean I don't know what I'm doing."

"No, I'm good." I can't imagine one-on-one girl time with any-one. Not now that Riley is gone.

"Are you going to give him your number?" She stands on tiptoe and peers over the door. "He looks like a decent guy. Friendly. Handsome."

"Not a chance. That's the last thing I need."

She flicks her hair over her shoulder. "I think you'll find you're wrong. But I'm not judging."

·········

Later that evening, after the café has closed and we've locked up the shop, I drive to the gym. It's one of those twenty-four-hour places that is only open twenty-four hours certain days of the week, but it works well for me, even though I'm not working out. It's cheap. I take a quick shower, washing away the smell of coffee that clings to my hair and skin. It's not an unpleasant smell, but it gets old after a while. I fill up my water bottle at the fountain and wave at the girls at the front desk as I leave. They're getting to know me. I wonder what they call me? Shower Girl, maybe? But it doesn't matter. I pay to use the facilities, and I'd still take a shower if I *did* work out.

After picking up some takeout, Thai today because I've had burgers almost everyday this week, I drive around town aimlessly. I liked the Walmart parking lot. It felt safe, even if it was bright and sometimes noisy. I debate my options. I could stay within town where people can see my car—which is good safety-wise, but bad for keeping a low profile—or I could drive a short distance from town and listen to the waves. Despite the missing woman, Salvation Hills seems safe enough. It's small and neighbourly. So I decide on the latter. It could save me the embarrassment of being seen. I don't need anyone else I know to see me sleeping in my car.

There's a parking lot a short drive out of town. It has a boardwalk that goes along the top of the hills, looking out to sea. I drive there and park near the edge that overlooks the water. The water gleams under a sun that is lowering itself to the horizon beyond the hills behind me. It'll be dark soon. Far below, waves crash against the rocky shore, their roar muted by the brisk wind and the rustling grass. The air is crisp and smells faintly of ocean, sea grass, and green, forested hills. I sit on the hood of my car and eat my takeout, then lean back against the windshield to watch the clouds turn a rosy pink as the sun sets. Red skies at night...

Before I get ready for bed, I play around on my phone, simply enjoying being alone and in nature. The sound of the waves is soothing. My hoodie is warm enough that I don't mind sitting outside in the dark, rather than rolled up in my sleeping bag inside the stuffy car. I scroll through social media. I'm no longer active and have turned off location services, but I like to see what my old classmates are up to. It seems like they've happily graduated and gotten on with their lives. I'm surprised to see that one of the girls in my class, Jessica, is planning her wedding. She's only been out of high school a couple months. I push down the gut-wrenching jealousy that sours my stomach at the thought of missing out. I don't really care about these people. Never did. They didn't care about me either. Riley was my mainstay, my anchor. And she's long gone.

A Salvation Hills news story pops up. I almost scroll past it, when a familiar picture catches my eye. I click on the video and listen to the newscast.

"Authorities report that Vanessa Wilson, the woman reported missing late last week, did not leave town voluntarily. Evidence points to her having been taken by force. The Salvation Hills chief of police released more information about the apparent abduction at a press conference this afternoon."

I listen to the press conference, dread growing in my belly. The police chief doesn't go into detail, but warns residents of Salvation Hills to report any strange activity to the police. He mentions that women living alone should be cautious if opening their doors to strangers.

I quickly close out of the article. I don't need all that in my head right before I go to sleep.

More nervous than normal, I brush my teeth, rinse with a sip from my water bottle, then fold down the backseat so I can lay out the foam mattress and sleeping bag I use as a bed. It's not as comfortable as a real bed, but it works. The backseat folds up for daytime, hiding my strange sleeping arrangement from prying eyes, when I remember to do it. I place the black poster boards I've cut to fit my windows and unfold the sun screen that goes inside the windshield. It's not perfect. Light still comes in if I'm parked near a streetlamp, and I assume light escapes if I'm playing on my phone or using my flashlight inside the car, but it gives me a bit of privacy and lets me sleep without anyone being able to watch me.

At least, anyone who isn't dead.

Riley sits in the passenger seat, her black-booted foot propped on my dashboard. She leans her head back against the headrest, turning to face me.

"Sweet dreams," she says, her eyes luminous in the darkness, wide and sad.

I ignore her, closing my eyes and focusing on my breathing. This can't be normal, can it? Still seeing your dead best friend a year after they died? I should be over it by now, shouldn't I?

Somehow, I drift off to sleep.

··········

I startle awake, nearly clocking my head on the ceiling of my car as I bolt upright. It's pitch black, the air cold and moist with condensation. I rub my eyes, then peer into the darkness, listening for what woke me. Outside, the wind rustles the grass and the waves break on the shore below. Nothing seems out of place, but *something* woke me. What if it's whoever took the missing woman? Maybe I should have risked sleeping at the Walmart again instead of coming up here.

"What do you think that was?" Riley asks from the front seat. She's looking at her fingernails, bored.

"I don't know. I was sleeping." I reach for my phone, but it's not where I left it. I feel around in the dark. Finally, my fingers close around its hard shell in the space between the seat and the floor. It must have fallen while I was asleep. I fish it out, almost dropping it again, and turn on the flashlight. I tilt the light to the ceiling as I listen to the night.

"So you're talking to me now?"

"No. You're not real. I'm talking to myself. Be quiet."

"That hurts, you know." She gropes at her heart with both hands. Dramatic. *"I'm wounded. Of course I'm real."*

I shake my head. I am seriously losing it. I should go to a therapist. Or see a doctor. Get some meds, a CAT scan, something. Not that I can afford any of those options. Or the consequences that might come with them.

There's a shout nearby. I flip over my phone, hiding the light as I tap the screen to turn off the flashlight. My heart pounds against my ribs, loud in my ears.

"What was that?"

"That's what woke you," Riley says, disappearing into the darkness at the exact moment I want her company.

Chapter Two

"Thanks a lot," I mutter to Riley's ghost, wherever she's gone. I peel back my poster-board privacy screen, but can't see through the fog of condensation on the window.

The shouting outside the car continues, but it sounds more like fun conversation than murder. It's not close. I lie back down, but my bladder twinges. I won't be able to sleep until I pee, not now that I'm awake. Middle of the night bathroom breaks are the worst when you live in your car.

I grab my keys from the cupholder, slip on my flip-flops, and climb out the back door. The air is moist, scented with brine and damp earth. Below me, the surf roars along the rocks and the grass rustles in the breeze. The shouts have subsided. The moon and stars hide behind clouds, making the night darker than usual. I tend to my business in the dark.

The shouting starts again before I pull my sweats up. They sound excited, if not quite happy. Lights flash in the field behind me, bobbing about and moving like flashlights. I wonder what's going on. The clock on my phone says it's almost one in the morning. I lock my car and slip my keys into my bra. I'm going to find out.

The grass in the field is tall enough to brush my waist as I creep through it. I test the ground with my toe before each step. I'm scared of what might hide in the grass—snakes or a skunk? Or maybe an overgrown ditch or well? If I fall into some hole way out here, I wouldn't be found until it was too late. Thankfully, I'm wrong on all counts. The field transitions into grass that's only a few inches tall. Someone has mowed it recently.

Beyond me, glowing palely in the darkness, is the back of a dilapidated farmhouse. Part of the roof is missing. Stairs that once led to the lopsided verandah have fallen to pieces. The windows and empty doorway gape black, like the eye sockets of a skull. The lights that had been in the field earlier have moved inside. A beam of light bobs around on the second floor. Whoever's in the house is quiet right now. Only the roar of the ocean and the incessant chirp of crickets fills the darkness. Who could be in the house? And what am I thinking, traipsing out here in the middle of the night? This is probably a drug deal or some other nonsense I should stay far, far away from. I'm about to hurry back to my car when there's another excited shout. This doesn't sound like a drug deal—not that I know what that sounds like.

I creep around the outside of the ruined structure, sticking to the shadows. I won't go in. I couldn't if I wanted to. The steps back here are impassable. If the outside of the house is this rough, it can't be safe inside. Why are there people here, at this hour? I must be going crazy, because I continue around the perimeter.

The front is a little better than the back, though barely. Paint is peeling off the wooden door and the steps are crooked and warped. But at least there *is* a door. And steps. A dark SUV sits in the overgrown drive. No one is in the car or waiting outside. Curious, I peer in the window. Fast food wrappers litter the floor, and the backseat is a mess of backpacks and sweaters, giving me no clue who these people are or what they're doing.

Someone screams.

I whirl towards the house. Thundering footsteps reverberate from inside. They'll see me! I run around the vehicle, making a beeline for the grass. Before I can reach it, the front door bursts open with a squeal of protest, and three breathless people spill out. It's too dark to see their faces. We freeze, staring at each other. Then the one in front lets out another high-pitched shriek.

I take off like a scared rabbit, racing around the house and darting into the tall grass, the undulating tips hiding the path of my retreat.

......

"Late night?" Claire asks.

I stop wiping the table I've been cleaning for who knows how long. "What?"

Claire pours milk into the frother and steams it, then tamps down espresso grinds, and brews a triple shot. She pours the espresso into a mug, tops it with four pumps of hazelnut syrup and pours the milk over top, expertly drawing a heart with the froth. She sets the mug in front of me.

"Drink. You're falling asleep on your feet. What were you doing last night? *Not* sleeping, obviously."

I can't tell her the truth without admitting that I'm living in my car, so I shrug. "Yeah. I couldn't sleep."

It's not a lie. After I made it back to my car, I got paranoid about the trio from the house following me or driving down to the lot, so I drove back to town and found an inconspicuous spot on a residential street. By that time, I was wide awake, and soon the sun peeked over the horizon and ruined any remaining hope of sleep. I'd gone to the closest fast-food restaurant for some breakfast instead.

"Something on your mind? Want to talk about it?"

I shake my head. Claire's nice. She's always trying to get to know me, even though I never volunteer information. If I was being honest about who I am, and if I was planning to stay here long term, I think we could be friends, despite our age difference. Claire is Heather's friend. They're both in their late thirties.

"Claire, can you give me a hand?" Heather calls from the kitchen.

"You good?" She touches my shoulder. I nod and she disappears into the back. Faint laughter filters out of the kitchen. It must be nice working with your best friend.

The door jingles. I set my coffee down in the staff beverage area and turn to greet our customers. My cheeks flare with heat. It's the redheaded guy and his two friends from yesterday. I stare at them a moment. There's something else...

The redheaded guy lets out a short, high-pitched laugh in response to something the taller guy says. That's when it hits me. They were the people in that abandoned house last night. Heat creeps up my neck. I hope they don't recognize me.

I clear my throat and force a smile. "Morning. Welcome to The Roasted Bean."

A frown creases the redhead's forehead, while the girl with purple hair lights up. She raises her eyebrows and smiles at me. I think she recognizes me. I bite my lip to hide my grimace. The redhead holds up a finger, pointing at me, before using it to tap his lips. I think he's trying to place me, only his brain isn't making the connection. I hope he doesn't. I hope none of them do. How mortifying would that be?

"Are you okay?" I ask, hoping to distract him. He's staring blankly at me, a slight frown creasing his forehead.

The pretty girl with the purple hair pushes past him. She grins at me, her dark brown eyes crinkling. "He's fine, probably just overwhelmed with all the beverage options. I'll have a half-sweet, salted caramel latte. With an extra shot of espresso. It was an exhausting night, ya know."

She says this with meaning, as though expecting me to confirm I was the weirdo in the field.

"Sure," I say simply, tapping in her order. A frown crinkles her forehead, and she purses her lips like she's disappointed by my response. She steps aside, giving the tall, dark-haired guy space at the counter.

"Black dark roast," he says, in a bored monotone.

"Room for cream?"

"No."

Bitter, black coffee it is then. The drink suits him.

"Mase, what do you want?" the girl asks.

Mase, the copper-haired guy, is still frowning at me, though he's put his finger away—both hands are now shoved in the front pockets of his tight jeans.

"Uh, I don't know. What do you recommend?"

I shrug. "Everything's good. My favourite is anything hazelnut, usually a latte."

"Allergic." He grimaces, then says, contemplatively, "I guess I'll have a large... non-fat... half-sweet... double shot..."

He trails off of listing practically every modification, skimming the chalkboard beverage menu above me, his gaze dropping to my face periodically.

"What's wrong with you?" I ask, before remembering customer service is my job. I literally bite my tongue. The quick burst of pain distracts me from blushing further.

The girl snickers, covering her mouth with her hand, her eyes dancing between Mase and me. Even the somber, dark-haired guy's mouth quirks upward into what might be a smirk.

Mase shakes his head, a quick jerk of denial. "Nothing. I'll have the salted caramel latte, too."

"Non-fat, half-sweet, double shot of espresso?"

He blinks a few times, red creeping up his neck. "Uh… yeah."

"Great." I key in his order. "That'll be sixteen fifty-two."

"Mason's paying," the dark-haired guy says, jerking his thumb towards Mason, whose cheeks are now as red as mine felt when he first walked in. He takes the girl's arm and they walk across the room to a table near the window. They sit so close together that I can tell they're a couple.

Mason passes me a twenty. "Keep the change."

"Thanks."

"I get it, now. I know where I saw you!"

"Here?" I ask, inwardly cringing.

He leans against the counter and, low enough so his friends can't hear, says, "It was you, wasn't it?"

"What are you talking about?" My fingers fumble as I fish out the correct change for the tip jar.

"Last night. At the Becker house. Did you have fun sneaking around?"

"I—what? I didn't… What's the Becker house?"

"You know." He smirks, then pushes off the counter to join his friends.

I grimace, taking a deep breath and go to make their drinks. There's no doubt these three were in that old house last night, but why? I wish they hadn't recognized me. It's so weird that I snuck up on them and almost creepier that I ran away. My stomach churns with nerves and embarrassment. But I have no reason to be embarrassed. I was checking out a weird noise in the middle of the night. It makes sense that I'd run away from three strangers. That's logical. What isn't logical is that I thought it was a good idea to traipse through an overgrown field and head towards shouting in the middle of the night. Yep. I'm stupid.

"He likes you," Riley says, leaning against the counter beside me. I shoot her a look but say nothing. I'm at work and she isn't real. Besides, she abandoned me last night when I could've really used her company. She rolls her eyes at me, then looks pointedly across the café at Mason. It doesn't matter if he likes me or not, because I'm not putting down roots of any sort in Salvation Hills.

Drink tray in hand, I force myself to walk over to the group.

Mason taps his phone screen. "It's clearly an orb."

His friend, arm over Purple's shoulder, shrugs. "It's dust. Clearly."

"Oh, come on. Its ghostly energy!"

Purple smiles at me, reaching for the coffee cup I pass her. I set the other two down on the table, straining to see the phone screen without being too obvious.

"You into ghosts?" Dark-hair asks. "Is that why you were creeping about our car last night? Or were you trying to break into it?"

"Seriously?" I put the hand that isn't holding the tray on my hip. "I don't want your crappy car. I've got my own."

"Your own crappy car?" He raises an eyebrow.

I can't tell if he's teasing or accusing me. He doesn't know what I drive. And I *like* my car. Besides, Riley and I went everywhere in that thing: the mall, skinny dipping at midnight, falling asleep while parked in front of her house because neither of us really wanted to go home. It was our own little piece of freedom. I wouldn't give it up for the world.

"You should join us," Mason says. "On a hunt, I mean."

"A ghost hunt," Purple corrects. "You make it sound like we're killing things."

I laugh nervously. "I don't think so. I don't know you guys."

Mason points at himself, then his friends. "I'm Mason Evans, that's Conrad Taylor—he looks mean, but he's not. And last but not least is Bethany Morgan, our own personal sunshine."

"Bethy," she says. "Now you know us. Who are you?"

"Riley Miller." The name falls from my lips with ease. It should, after using it for a year.

"So, you want to join us?" Mason asks.

I bite the inside of my lip, glancing at the seat beside Mason, where Riley's sitting. She rests her head in her hand, elbow propped on the table. Maybe joining them will help me get over whatever is making me see her all the time. "What are you trying to do by ghost hunting?"

"Get evidence of ghosts. Prove they exist."

"Or prove they *don't* exist," Conrad says dryly.

"Our resident skeptic." Bethy rests her head on his shoulder, beaming up at him.

"All right. I'll try it out if you promise you're not weirdos."

Bethy laughs. "I can't promise that. But we're *nice* weirdos."

"Tomorrow night," Mason says, leaning over the table and rubbing his hands together. "We're investigating the Turner house on

Highland Road. One of the original houses of Salvation Hills. Give me your number and I'll add you to the group chat."

I recite my number, while glancing at Riley. This might be some weird ploy for Mason to get it, but I need to know if I'm crazy or if ghosts really exist. I'm sure I'm losing it... but what if I'm not? That thought numbs me to the core.

"Great. We'll text you with the plan and again when we're on our way to the house. Unless you want to ride with us?"

I shake my head. I'm not that crazy. "Send me the address and I'll meet you there."

"Cool." Mason grins at me and my stomach twists with something that's not quite anticipation.

··········

That night I stay in the gym's parking lot and piggyback off their Wi-Fi to save my data. Once I had the trio's full names, it was easy to track them down online. They've got a video channel dedicated to ghost hunting called *Cracks in the Veil.*

With my phone plugged into the power bank I charge daily at work, I scroll through their videos, choosing the ones that seem the least scary. Mason goofs off a lot. He's demanding and loud. If anyone's going to scream in terror, it's him. I rarely see Conrad, though I hear his voice. He must man the cameras. Bethy is the stoic star of the show, countering Mason's theatrics with common sense and empathy, though I catch her fixing her hair several times.

Overall, they seem happy and sincere, like a close group of friends. I'm wary of all of it.

"Are you really going to do this?" Riley asks, from her usual spot in the passenger's seat. *"It doesn't seem like you."*

I roll onto my back, holding my phone above my head.

"You can't ignore me forever. I'm your best friend, you know."

I close my eyes. "Riley, you're gone. You're not real. Can you please give me some space?"

"I don't know why you keep saying that. I'm as real as I ever was."

"No, you're not." I set my phone aside and stare at the gray fabric of the ceiling. "You're dead. I watched them bury you."

I can feel Riley roll her eyes. Of course I can. She's generated by my imagination. Maybe ghost hunting will be my new hobby and take my mind off my loss. Maybe this will be healing.

I roll over, searching the car for Riley, but she's disappeared. I close my eyes. My head hurts with unshed tears. How long am I supposed to miss her?

This is why I can't go home. Well, partly. The other reason is because I don't fit in there. I never have. Riley helped me, was an outcast like me. Together, we were so strong. Now I'm alone, simply existing. No one gets me. I'm the lone weirdo. It sucks.

Here's to another exhausting night, existing on the fringe of society.

·····•·•····

The next day, Friday, I'm at the café when my phone pings. I've been added to the group chat, and a picture of the house we'll be investigating fills my screen. It's a large, pleasant-looking colonial house, like many of the homes here in Salvation Hills. The shutters are painted a fresh navy; the rest of the house is white. It looks expensive—well-maintained and happily lived-in, with bright flowers growing in beds around the front of the house. Mason's text under the picture reads: *Built in 1813. Let's hope it's haunted!*

Conrad texts back while I'm looking at it: *Probably not.*

Should I bring anything? I type, and hit send.

Mason replies. *Yourself, your phone and a sweater. We might be outside for a while.*

I send a thumbs up emoji. It's only noon and my palms are already clammy—for more than one reason. Not only am I nervous about this ghost hunting business—what if it's real and I really am haunted by my best friend?—but I'm also nervous about getting close to these three. I don't know them. This could be some elaborate trap, a trio of serial killers luring in their next victim. But I don't really think so. Not after watching their videos. That would be *way* too elaborate of a scheme.

The bell above the door dings and several of our regulars drop in for the lunch rush, looking for a quick meal and another cup of caffeine to keep them going through the rest of their workdays. Before I know it, I'm wiping down tables so we can finish the dishes before we close.

"Any plans for the weekend?" Claire asks, carrying in a box of groceries.

"Is Heather back? I'll help." I hurry to the back and grab a box of supplies. Heather takes the weekends off and two college kids man the shop in her absence. Apparently, they've been doing it for the past several summers.

"So?" Claire asks, grabbing the last box out of the back of Heather's SUV. We stack these on the kitchen workbench.

"'So' what?"

"Plans?"

"Actually, yeah. I'll be hanging out with some friends tonight."

Heather rounds the corner in time to hear this. "Riley has plans? I don't believe it."

She holds her hand out for a fist bump. I hold back an eye roll and give her a light tap with my fist.

"I'm glad," she says. "You deserve to relax and have fun. Do you want to take off early?"

I shake my head. No point leaving until it's time to head to the house. "No. I'm good."

My phone buzzes. Heather and Claire exchange looks.

"Is that your *friend*?" The way Claire emphasizes friend implies she thinks I have a date.

I pull my phone out of my back pocket, heat creeping up my neck. Mason has sent a text that reads: *We're heading to the house now. 216 Highland Road.*

"I think that's a yes," Heather says. "Go. You only have an hour left. I'll pay you for it."

I grip my phone tighter, tears welling in my eyes. "Thanks."

"There's supposed to be a storm tonight, be safe," Claire calls after me. "And have fun!"

I don't know why they're so nice to me.

On my way. I send the message and grab my backpack with the change of clothes I'd packed for tonight.

Moments later I'm changed and in my car, heading slowly uphill towards Highland Road, my stomach churning with nerves.

Chapter Three

Katherine Turner:
1796-1864

I will never forget the first time I saw this cursed house. It's burnt into my memory like a brand. I was so hopeful then, young, impressionable. My husband was such a powerful man, with land and money. My life was going to be grand. He'd helped me out of the carriage. I'd taken his arm and looked up at the beautiful house before me, on the wide swathes of land that would be our livelihood. Before all this grandeur, I'd felt so tiny and young. I was to be the mistress of it all. I'd felt lucky.

It didn't take long to break me of these illusions.

My husband lashed out in violence that very night. I'd cowered before him, knowing my duties as a wife, but something had upset him and he had to let his anger out on someone. I was the easiest target. My life was a downward spiral from there.

I did everything I could to please him. I bore him children, twelve in total. I watched as only a handful survived, grieving in silence the ones I lost.

Twenty-five years after our marriage, my sixth child, lovely Prudence, with her whole life ahead of her, was carried into the house, bloodied and limp. She was the one who broke me. I knew, I just knew her death was Joseph's fault. My grief allowed me to voice my accusations. They nearly had me killed.

I bore no more children after Prudence's untimely death, though the years with Joseph carried on.

When he finally died, I rejoiced. I laughed at his funeral. The guests whispered behind their hands that I'd gone mad with grief. But I had never felt such relief. After thirty-seven years of hell, I was finally free. But not free of the house. No, I will never be free of this house.

· · · · ● · ● · · ·

Present Day

The house looms before me, framed by towering oak trees, their limbs hanging over the front lawn. It's the last house on the road and it's far enough away from the others that it feels isolated. The driveway looks like original cobblestones, worn in the centre from centuries of wheels. I pull in behind the navy SUV that I recognize from the other night. I wonder who it belongs to. Probably Conrad. He seems the most responsible. Mason or Bethy would probably drive something flashier. Or junkier. I haven't figured Mason out yet. A van I don't recognize is parked beside the SUV. I can't picture Mason or Bethy driving it. It must belong to whoever lives here.

I lock my car behind me, and pause for a moment to take in the view. The house sits near the top of the hill, looking out over what would have been empty fields, once upon a time. Now the town's houses and businesses cover the hills. Beyond these, the ocean gleams silver in the late afternoon sunshine. Heavy gray clouds gather on the horizon, but they're so far away they aren't threatening.

"Riley!" Mason calls from the front door. He's dressed in jeans and a hoodie, casual like me. At least I'm dressed appropriately.

I make my way towards him, sudden shyness almost overwhelming me. There's an older man and woman standing just outside the open door with Mason, Conrad, and Bethy. Bethy has her amethyst hair pulled up and a full face of makeup. Conrad looks as cool as ever in a denim jacket and tee. The older couple are composed and well-dressed in wrinkle free clothes that probably cost more than my meagre paycheque. I'm a little embarrassed for them to see me in my holey jeans and flannel shirt with a naked face. I shouldn't be. Riley would toss her head and stride past them, but I duck my chin shyly instead.

"These are the Lees. They're the current owners of the house and the ones letting us investigate."

Figures. They look like they could afford a place like this. I peer past them into a tidy front entry. The late afternoon sun shines off the polished hardwood floors, making the place bright and cheerful. A set of double doors are open, beyond them is a comfortable living room. Despite the house being old, it doesn't *look* like it should be haunted, but I guess we'll see.

I hold out my hand to the Lees, like my parents taught me. "It's nice to meet you."

Mrs. Lee smiles at me, her face softening with the expression. "It's nice to meet you as well. The others were just telling us a bit of what you'll be doing here. I hope you all can give us some sort of peace."

"I hope so too." I murmur, with no idea what to say or what might be in store for me. Isn't ghost hunting just wandering around asking an empty room for signs, measuring changes in air temperature and stuff? How is any of that going to help the Lees?

"Well, we'll be off," Mr. Lee says. He yells up the stairs. "Eric, Audrey, let's go!"

Light footsteps race down the stairs, and two kids run through the front hall, past us, and out the front door. The older kid stops on the steps to look back at us. She's probably about fourteen, with glossy black hair that Riley would have killed for.

"Good luck with the ghosts," she says, smirking. I can't tell if she's being cheeky or sincere. Still, a shiver runs down my spine.

"You have my number if you need to call," Mr. Lee says. "There's supposed to be a storm this weekend. The fuse box is in the utility room, next to the washing machine. Call if you need anything."

"Will do," Conrad says, his voice calm and level. I would trust him with my two-hundred-year-old house if I had one. He seems responsible. Slightly scary, but responsible.

Mr. Lee hesitates on the steps, looking up at the house, his brow furrowed with concern, until his wife touches his arm. He smiles and nods at her.

We all stand on the verandah and watch the family pile into their van and back out of the driveway. We wave as they disappear down the road.

"What do we do first?" I ask.

"Set up the cameras." Conrad strides across the grass to the SUV and pulls out cases of equipment. He places them on the steps of the verandah. "We'll cover as much of the house as we can. We've got four stationary cameras and a few handhelds, plus our phones. If we're not getting anything, we can move the stationary ones around after a while. Let's go."

I'm pretty useless with setting up tech, so I mostly hang out at the front of the house and wait for someone to tell me what to do. They don't order me around, but it doesn't take them long to set up. Soon we're seated on the porch swing, which moves crookedly out of time. The beam overhead creaks. The breeze is scented with green growing things and damp earth. It carries with it the chatter of happy birds.

"What are we waiting for?" I ask. "Sundown?"

Mason grins at me and puts his arm over the back the swing. I try not to flinch, but can't help stiffening as he brushes my shoulders. "Is this your first time ghost hunting?"

"Yes. Why?"

"You don't need darkness for ghostly activity. There can be just as much evidence in the daylight."

"So why do it in the dark at all?"

"It's way more fun."

Bethy nods in agreement, but Conrad stares stoically forward.

"Still," Mason goes on, "I think apparitions are easier to spot at night. It's quieter. And I think the temperature is more stable, without sunlight and air-con." He kicks at the floorboards of the verandah, wrenching the swing out of time again.

"Okay, so why are we sitting out here?" I ask.

"We're waiting for Nat," Conrad says.

"Who's Nat?"

Mason's arm creeps closer to me. "Natasha Patino. She's a medium we work with sometimes. She's in her thirties, but she's still cool."

"Excuse me?" Conrad asks. "Careful what you say, give it a few years and you'll be there."

Bethy elbows him. "You're only upset because you're almost there."

He scowls. "Am not. Twenty-four is six whole years from thirty."

"True. Dating you would be weird if you were that old." She mock shudders. "And it's nine years for me, so you'll be there a lot sooner, old man."

So they're twenty-one and twenty-four. A bit older than me, but close enough maybe we can be friends. I think of Heather and Claire. They're in their thirties and there's nothing wrong with them. "What's wrong with people in their thirties? It's not like they're old. You're not old until you're in your fifties, at least."

"Would you date a thirty-year-old?" Mason asks.

That's a simple question. The true answer is no, I wouldn't date anyone. Not right now. Not for a long time. I don't want to risk it. I channel my inner Riley, tilting my chin up defiantly. "Depends on who it is."

The distant roar of an engine fills the air. A blue motorcycle speeds up the hill and turns smoothly into the driveway. The driver is wearing a black leather jacket and jeans that cling to compact, athletic curves.

"There's Nat," Conrad says, standing. Bethy follows suit and takes his arm. I rise too, suddenly nervous.

Nat takes off her helmet and shakes out curly, shoulder-length black hair, before grinning across the lawn at us. Even at this distance, with the setting sun playing against her features, the red stain of her lips contrasts nicely with her olive skin. She might be in her thirties, but she's gorgeous, as confidently beautiful as Bethy, but in a totally different way. I shove my hands in my pockets and look at the ground near my feet, shy again. I wish I was more like Riley. Or Bethy and Nat.

"Hello, all," Nat says, striding across the grass, a small backpack slung over one shoulder. She looks at me quizzically, her eyes roving over me as though taking everything in at once and actually seeing me as me, and not the person I'm pretending to be. Not that I'm doing great at that. I shift from foot to foot under her appraisal. "This must be Riley."

I take her proffered hand limply, nothing like the strong shake I offered Mr. and Mrs. Lee. "Hi."

She grips my fingers warmly, but her eyes skim over me and seem to catch on something behind me. She stares over my shoulder for a beat too long. Her lips curve slightly up at the edges, and she lets me go. I turn to see what she was looking at. Riley—ghost Riley—sits on the bench beside Mason, leaning against his arm. She waves at me coyly. I can't help but smile at the image of a ghost snuggling into a ghost hunter without his knowledge. But then my chest tightens. If Nat is a medium and can see Riley—if that *is* what she was looking at—that means Riley isn't a figment of my imagination. It means she's really here and not resting in peace. It means I need to help her. She can't be here. She's not supposed to be living my messed-up life with me, not now. Not anymore. Maybe Nat can help. I'll have to press her for information without giving away any of my own. I run a hand through my hair in frustration.

"What do you think, Nat? Will our recruit be any good?" Mason asks.

She shrugs and sits on the edge of the verandah, leaning against a post, with one leg folded under the other. "We'll have to see what she's made of. I think she'll have a way with spirits. I think they'll like her."

If that isn't confirmation that she saw my ghost, nothing is, but then she continues. "She's so cute and tiny, with those pretty blue eyes, anyone would like her. Wouldn't they, Mase?"

Mason flushes red. "I've changed my mind. I don't think we need you on this investigation, Nat. Why don't you head home now?"

"And miss all the fun? You know I like fireworks."

Mason heaves a put-upon sigh and fishes his phone out of his pocket. "If you're not leaving, do you want to hear the history of the house?"

"We all do," Bethy says. "Where are the handhelds?"

Conrad looks around. "In the car, I think. I'll grab one."

He strides across the lawn, circling behind the SUV. A car door slams before he reappears. He pauses, looking at my car. I squirm in my seat. Did I remember to put my pillow and everything in the trunk? I can't remember.

Conrad hurries back to us. Bethy sits back on the bench, running her hands through her hair and grinning. From the videos I've seen, I know she likes to be on camera and it seems she plans to be in as much of this video as possible.

"Got it," he says, adjusting the camera. "We're recording."

Mason turns to me. "We try to record everything once we start an investigation because you never know when something might happen."

Just then, there's a bang from inside the house.

"What was that?" Mason jumps to his feet and runs through the still-open front door. Bethy and I follow him, with Nat close behind. Conrad brings up the rear with the camera.

The double doors to the living room are both closed. Mason pushes on them lightly, but they're latched shut. He turns the handles and opens both doors at the same time. They're heavy, and swing open slowly. The room is exactly how we left it—nothing's out of place.

"We left these open, right?" Conrad asks.

Bethy nods. "One hundred percent. Why would we close them? We have a camera set up at the end of the hall to catch the supposed apparition. Maybe we caught the doors closing?"

Mason shakes his head, but strides over to the camera. "We hadn't started to record yet."

He powers the camera on and adjusts the angle. "Let's turn them all on now, even though it's still dusk. It'll be full dark soon enough."

Conrad, Mason and Bethy disappear to turn on the other three stationary cameras. I lean against the wall and point my gaze at my feet, but really, I'm watching Nat through my eyelashes, trying not to be obvious in my study of her. She's much more blatant in her study of me. Sitting on the stairs, arms propped on her knees, she stares at me. She opens her mouth to say something, then glances at the camera. She purses her lips, staying silent. Footsteps come down the stairs and Mason reappears.

"Did anything happen?" he asks.

"No," I say.

"Nat, do you sense anything?"

She stands up, brushing off the seat of her jeans, and paces the hall. "There's certainly an energy here, but it's elusive, like it's hiding from us."

"Maybe we just need to get it comfortable with us," Bethy says, returning with Conrad right behind her. To the house, she says, "I'm Bethy, and this is Conrad."

"I'm Mason. We don't mean you any harm. We're here to find out what happened in the past and to give the family who lives here some peace of mind. You've been scaring them."

He nods at me, indicating it's my turn. It seems idiotic to talk to a house, but I do it anyway. "I'm Riley. I guess I'm new at this, so please don't scare me too badly."

"I'm Nat. If you want to show yourself to me, I can see you and help you if that's what you need. You can interact with us for the night, but you can't follow us home."

My stomach drops. "They can do that?"

She straightens a picture on the wall. "Spirits can attach to people as easily as places."

I scan the room, but I can't see Riley anywhere. I hope she *is* a figment of my imagination after all. For her sake, she has to be.

"Let's get the history done, in case anything else happens." Conrad turns on the handheld camera again, centring the attached light on Mason. The entryway is dim, with only the light from the camera. The sun has mostly set and the windows are dark. It will only get darker as the night goes on. I shiver with fear, but also anticipation.

"Okay. So this is the Turner House, or the House on Highland Road. It was built before Salvation Hills was a town and the land surrounding it all belonged to Joseph Turner. He built the house, or more likely had it built, in 1813. I don't think he'd do the work himself. He doesn't seem like that kind of guy. He had a bunch of slaves and indentured servants, so I expect they were the ones to build it. In 1814 he married his wife, Katherine. They had twelve children—"

"Wait a second," Bethy asks. "Twelve?"

"Yeah—"

"That's way too many. Can you imagine how burnt-out that poor woman was?" She grimaces at Nat and me. "Ouch."

"Only five survived."

"That's even worse. All that work and stress and less than fifty percent live? That's like... a failing grade."

"Can I continue?"

She nods and zips her mouth shut. She doesn't throw away the key.

"Two of their kids lived to adolescence before dying, but the girl, Prudence died of blunt force trauma at fourteen, and her younger brother killed himself at eighteen. Their eldest surviving son, Philip, inherited the house. He had three children. Only two survived."

"Three's more like it," Bethy mutters. Mason shoots her a look.

"Philip's wife died in childbirth and he remarried. His second wife died inexplicably a few years later. No one knows what killed her, but she was supposedly a terrible stepmother. Rumour has it, and I agree, that the kids killed her. Maybe the husband. However she died, it wasn't natural."

Overhead, footsteps thump against the floorboards, stopping Mason's monologue. Mason looks at us, wide-eyed.

"We're alone, right?" Conrad asks.

"Yeah. It's private property and the family is gone," Mason says. "Who else could it be?"

Conrad shrugs. "Just checking."

"Could the Lees have come back?" I ask.

I open the front door, but only our vehicles are parked out front. It's now fully dark. The sky is heavy with clouds and the tree branches keep what little light the moon and stars emit from reaching the house. Someone could have parked in the shadows on the street and snuck in, but that's doubtful.

"There's only the front and back doors, and they both lead into the house. We can see them," Bethy says, a quaver of fear in her voice. "We have to be alone in the house."

"Let's go check it out." Conrad motions for us to go first. I don't know if he's lucky to be holding the camera, so he doesn't have to go first, or if he's unlucky because he'll be last. I keep myself firmly in the middle. There's no way I'm going anywhere alone tonight.

We rush up the stairs. A table at the top of the stairs holds a vase of fake flowers. They look black and faded in the dusky light. The second floor spreads out like a "T" on either side of us, wide hallways with several doors on either side. It looks like the upstairs of any house, except the floors are original hardwood, stained a rich brown. It's creepy, almost unfathomable, to think of all the people who walked here.

"You guys take that side, Conrad and I will take this one." Mason urges Bethy, Nat, and I to the right, as he turns in the opposite direction.

"Really?" Bethy whines. "Conrad and I are a couple."

But she follows Nat and me down the hallway. I poke my head cautiously into the first bedroom. My fingers itch to flip the light switch, but, even as a noob, I know that would ruin the video footage. Besides, I don't want the internet to know I'm a chicken. I jerk the door away from the wall, check under the bed, then rifle through the closet, feeling along the back wall. I close the accordion closet door, leaving the room as I'd found it. There's no one in this room. Posters of modern boy bands and artists I don't know cover the walls and the bedspread is a frilly pink. Stuffed animals are lined up on the bed, with one flopped down face-first. Had it fallen by accident or had a ghost done that? I back out of the room, feeling intrusive, the hairs on the back of my neck prickling under invisible, watchful eyes.

Nat emerges from the last room on the right and Bethy steps out of the room across from me, shaking her head.

"All clear on this side," Nat calls to the boys.

"No one's here, either," Conrad says, his deep voice echoing through the quiet house.

"Over here, guys," Mason calls. "There's also the attic. The Lees mentioned hearing things from up there."

CHAPTER FOUR

Gracie Turner:
1854-1899

Dearest Sister,

I do hope you are doing well and look forward to your visit this Christmas.

There is something pressing on my heart that I wish to hear your thoughts on. I fear my dear husband, Philip Jr., and Caroline, his sister if you remember, are awfully close. They discuss thoughts and ideas I had hoped Philip Jr. might share with me, but they ignore my input entirely. Sometimes, I pass Caroline's room and hear lowered voices. It isn't my place to open the door, but I wonder.

Once, late at night, I awoke to find Philip Jr. out of bed. Worried that something might have happened, I donned my robe and entered the chilly halls of the house to search for him. He was leaving Caroline's room by candlelight and was shocked to find me awake.

Worst of all, dear sister, is that Caroline is now with child, confirmed by our family physician. But she never leaves the house. She never goes to town, not even on Sundays when we all go to church. Of course, she could have liaisons with a servant, but I worry that my husband and sister-in-law's relationship isn't all it should be.

Since my marriage, I have heard strange rumours. The town's ladies talk about the sudden death of Philip Jr. and Caroline's stepmother. Some suggest poison. These rumours have not been spoken to me directly, but I have overheard some, and my maid has filled me in further. Rumour says that brother and sister worked together to do their stepmother in. From what my husband has told me, she was not a pleasant woman. But to suggest they may have killed her! I do not know what to think, except perhaps this event brought them closer together.

I hope you can share your perspective upon your next visit. This is not something I can ask my husband about, for what if I am wrong?

Yours, with all my love,

Gracie

··········

Present Day

Mason leads us to the end of the hall. There's a little door on the left disguised as a wall. It opens onto a narrow staircase leading up. This seems to be the type of house with lots of hidden nooks and crannies; passages for servants to pass unseen. The thought is unnerving. Anyone could be spying on us from anywhere. And anyone in this house right now is probably a ghost. The rest of the house is decorated and obviously lived in, but the attic feels abandoned. The stairs creak as we ascend and my nose prickles with dust. The room at the top of the stairs is empty except for some boxes pushed up against the wall. It's clear that no one comes up here much.

"I think this is where the slaves or servants would have lived," Mason says.

The air is hot and thick up here, despite the lateness of the season and the coolness of the evening. The roof slants towards the floor. Three dormer windows look out over the front of the house and three more over the back. I can't imagine what it would have been like to live up here, with who knows how many other people all crammed together. If it's hot right now, it would have been unbearable in the middle of summer, and I don't even want to think about how cold it would've been in the winter. The temperature seems to drop several degrees, though my skin is clammy, and sorrow wells within me. I rub my face, pretending it's itchy, but really, I'm trying to banish the sudden tears pressing at the back of my eyes. Why do I want to cry?

"You okay?" Nat asks, her hand on my shoulder.

I nod. "It's kinda oppressive up here."

"Yes. There's definite energy up here, but I think it's residual, which is a relief. Though..."

"What?"

She shakes her head. "No, it must be residual. I sense something, but nothing concrete."

I'm glad. I want whoever lived up here to have peace. It would be awful to remain captive in this house. This attic isn't a place anyone should ever call home.

"Should we ask some questions and then work our way down?" Bethy asks. She holds up two palm-sized devices, one slightly smaller than the other.

"What are those?" I ask. I should probably know since I agreed to go ghost hunting, but I'm completely new to this. Aside from some scary movies and the couple of their *Cracks in the Veil* videos, I have watched nothing involving ghosts or ghost hunting at all.

"This one's an EMF detector." She turns on the smaller of the two devices, the one with a series of lights across one end, and waves it about. The light stays steady on a single green bar. "Next to things that contain power, it will flash, but if there's no power and it flashes, it means there could be something else with us."

"Or *someone* else," Mason says.

"The spirit box," Bethy continues, ignoring him, "makes an ungodly sound as it switches through radio frequencies. Supposedly, spirits can use these frequencies to make themselves heard. Sometimes you'll get a word, or a string of them, that you shouldn't be able to hear because the signal switches so quickly." She goes to hand the spirit box to Conrad, but he takes a step back.

"I thought you didn't believe in ghosts," Bethy says in a teasing tone.

"I don't. But that thing can be weird. And loud."

Bethy smiles at him, shaking her head, and puts the spirit box down on the dusty floor. This must be an old argument for them. She walks about the attic, running the EMF detector along the walls, ceiling and floor, testing for anomalies. There's a beam with a cable running across it and up into a hole in the ceiling. She passes the EMF detector over it. It lights up, beeping. "There are some power lines, but they're pretty obvious. Otherwise, we're good."

She comes back to stand with us, holding the EMF detector out in front of her. One green bar shines steadily.

"Is there anyone here that would like to talk with us?" Mason asks the room. "If you do, can you make the EMF detector—the thing in Bethy's hand—flash?"

We wait a few seconds. Ghost hunting seems like a lot of standing around and scaring yourself while waiting for something to happen. I shift, impatient. The light on the EMF detector flashes to yellow.

"Ooh!" Mason yells, jumping from foot to foot, while Bethy merely raises her eyebrows.

"Should we turn on the spirit box?" Bethy asks.

"Yeah, unless—Nat, are you getting anything?"

Nat stands beside me with her eyes closed. "There's someone here, but they're hiding from me. They don't want me to know who they are. They're afraid of something. I think it's a girl."

"A girl? Like the daughter who died?" I ask.

Nat shrugs. "Could be."

"But this is the servants' quarters," Bethy says. "The girl Mason mentioned was a member of the family. Why would she be up here?"

"If she's trying to hide from something… Can you tell, Nat?" Mason asks.

Nat sways slightly, as though fully absorbed in trance.

"No, I can't see what it is, but it's dark. Evil." She rubs her arms. "I don't like it."

Gooseflesh pebbles my arms, though the attic is stifling.

"Spirit box?" Mason asks.

Nat shakes her head. "Not up here. It's too disruptive."

"Flashlights then." Mason snaps his fingers in quick succession at Bethy.

Bethy sticks out her tongue at him, pocketing the spirit box, then reaches into Conrad's back pocket and pulls out two small flashlights. She slaps him on the butt with her free hand, then walks away and sets a flashlight on one side of the attic and the other a few feet away.

"The red flashlight means no and the blue means yes. Can you turn on the flashlight if you want to talk to us?"

We stand in silence for a couple seconds, before the blue flashlight flickers and turns on. I step back, bumping into Nat. She takes my hand and squeezes.

"Yes!" Mason shouts. He is very much into this. It was probably him I heard him shouting and screaming back at the house by the sea. "To confirm that's you, turn the flashlight off on the count of three. One, two, three."

The flashlight blinks off, leaving us in inky darkness.

"That's great!" Mason says, at a much louder volume than the quiet house warrants. "Are you Prudence Turner, the girl who was beaten to death on the grounds?"

There's a long moment where nothing happens, but then the blue flashlight flickers on.

"Great. Can you turn that off?"

It's not great. It's anything but. Some girl was murdered on the property two centuries ago. But the quick responses we're getting are frightening and impressive.

Mason continues. "Were you murdered?"

The blue flashlight turns on. We wait for it to turn off.

"Do you know who killed you?"

The red flashlight turns on.

Nat shudders, leaning heavily against me. Her breath wheezes out between clenched teeth.

"Nat? Are you all right?" I ask, wincing as her hand clenches mine tighter.

She gasps, then lets me go, leaning forward and sucking in air. "We are not alone. We're not meant to be here. There's someone else here."

"Who? What's here?" Bethy asks, her voice shaking with fear.

"What did you see, Nat?" Mason asks. Conrad steps around us, so the camera is on Nat's face.

She shakes her head, bracing her hands on her knees. "I'm not sure. It's still hiding from me, but the girl is gone. She's afraid of the darkness too. I don't think she was the girl who was murdered. At least, not the daughter of the original family."

Behind me, Bethy shrieks.

"What?" Mason asks.

"Something touched me. It felt like it brushed up against me." She shuffles closer to Nat and me.

A bang rattles through the floorboards, shaking the windows.

"What was that?" I ask, my voice weak.

Mason runs to the end of the attic and peers down the stairs. "The door is closed, guys."

"Really?" Conrad runs after him and goes down the stairs, his footsteps banging hollowly in the narrow staircase. "No way. Two separate doors closing on their own? It's got to be a draft or something."

Mason follows him down. "There's no air movement. If there was a draft, we could tell. Do you have the thermometer?"

"Back pocket."

"Don't you dare slap his ass." Bethy's voice shakes, though she says it lightheartedly. "That's off-limits to the likes of you."

"No worries. I'm not interested in it."

A few seconds go by. I can barely see them at the bottom of the stairs until Conrad turns the camera and the light from it momentarily blinds me.

"See? No change in temperature, and there's no draft."

"Can we leave the attic? It's scary." Bethy asks. She grabs the flashlights and hugs them to her chest.

"I agree," Nat says. She's been silent this whole time. "Whatever or whoever is up here really doesn't want us here."

"*Whatever*? What do you think it is?"

Nat shrugs. "It's hard to tell at this point. Probably the spirit of a deceased human, but it could be something else. It's angry."

At those words, I race down the stairs, my feet almost missing the steps. I'm not sticking around to meet an angry spirit—I need to get out of this attic. Conrad fumbles with the door. It has one of those tiny, old, oval doorknobs, stiff with age. The door creaks slowly open, and he rushes out, the rest of us right behind him.

The hallway is much cooler, though Mason's right—there is no draft. I can feel the hot air of the attic settling about my ankles, but it isn't blowing out enough for the door to have moved, let alone slammed shut. It makes no sense unless someone, living or dead, slammed it shut. And the only living people here are us.

The dark hallway isn't welcoming. In fact, it's spooky with its long shadows, but the oppressive tension I've been feeling since we went up to the attic is gone.

My fear gives way to anger. I am so gullible. "Did you guys rig this? If you did, it's not funny."

"How would we have rigged it?" Mason asks, indignant. "We were all up in the attic together. Do you want to go check for strings?"

I rub my arms, feeling even more scared by his response. I kind of do want to check for rigging, but I'm not going back up there alone. And... a part of me, one that's growing bigger by the second, knows he's telling the truth. "You mean... ghosts are real?"

"Absolutely." Nat puts a reassuring hand on my shoulder. "Even Conrad believes in them, though he'll deny it until he's given scientific proof."

"Which will be never." The unwavering calm of Conrad's voice soothes me, taking away the smallest bit of my fear. I don't know if I could be here if it wasn't for him and Nat.

"If you're not going to check for tricks, let's go down to the living room," Mason says. "I want to see if Nat can sense anything there."

"Why? What happened in the living room?" she asks warily.

"I'll tell you after."

It's a relief to put more distance between the attic and myself. I stick to the middle of the group as we make our way down the main staircase, listening intently for any strange sounds. The wind is picking up, howling around the outside of the house, hiding the small creaks that are common for an old house.

The living room is set up as a family room with a flat-screen TV mounted over a marble mantel. In the centre of the room, there's a large leather couch. The room still holds some of its historical charm, thanks to the tall ceilings and original mouldings.

An ancient chandelier hangs in the centre of the room, swaying slightly. But everything else has been thoroughly modernized. I wonder how the ghosts feel about that.

"Why is the chandelier swaying?" Bethy asks.

Conrad zooms the camera in on the chandelier. Its movement is almost imperceptible.

"Ooh... You're right," Mason says.

"Did us walking down the stairs make it move?" I ask.

"Another skeptic. Keep it up. Don't let these believers get to you," Conrad says with approval. "Run up and down the stairs and we'll find out."

"I'll come with you." Bethy tugs my sleeve as she passes. In the camera's light, her amethyst hair looks almost gray. I nod and follow her out of the room. She whispers, "I don't want to be alone in this house."

"Me neither. Is it usually this scary?" I'm not terrified, but I'm certainly not comfortable.

She shakes her head and runs up the stairs, taking them two at a time. I follow her, purposefully landing heavily on each step. At the top of the stairs, she answers my question. "We rarely get anything except cold spots and some EMF. Sometimes there's other activity, but not like here. No slamming doors and dark entities. There's something different about this house."

I don't want to believe in ghosts. I shiver and run back down the stairs. Bethy's footsteps, close behind my own, make my heart race as though I'm being chased. The guys are focused on the chandelier when I run back into the living room and come to a stop beside Nat, panting.

"You okay?" Nat asks me in a low voice.

I nod, shrugging. "This place is scary."

"I think you're sensitive as well. Have you ever seen anything?" She studies my face. All I can see of her is her skin, glowing palely in the dark. Her eyes hide in shadow until the light from the camera turns to us. I look to the guys without answering Nat.

"It moved when you came down the stairs, so probably nothing paranormal."

"Disappointing," Bethy says sarcastically.

"Okay, Nat. Stand in front of the mantel and tell me what you sense." Mason points from Nat to the fireplace, like a director.

She crosses the room. "Do you want me to touch it?"

"Do whatever you want."

She places a hand on the mantel. It's covered with framed pictures of the Lee family. There's a bouquet of fresh roses in a glass vase in the centre, faintly perfuming the room. Nat closes her eyes.

I struggle not to shift on my feet or turn around and look at the open doorway behind us. The hairs on the back of my neck stand up, so I focus on taking long, quiet breaths. Nat stays silently meditative for several long minutes. After a while, she speaks.

"It's strange. I can tell something bad happened here. My head hurts." She touches her temple. "Right here. But I can't see past the fog. Something's preventing me. *It's secret.*"

The last bit she whispers in a thin voice. Her brow furrows and she gasps. She jerks her hand off the mantel and looks around the room.

"There were deaths here. A husband and... wife? But their relationship was strained. They weren't... friendly." She speaks in a stilted voice, as though struggling to see through the veil between life and death. "I see two children, but they're not very nice. They're... I want to say evil. But that's not right. They're twisted somehow."

She shakes her head while rubbing her temple, finally looking at us. "My head hurts."

"Do you need to go outside?" I ask. I don't know if her head hurts because of what she's doing or because of the house. Either way, it makes me nervous. My stomach's twisting, and all the hairs on the back of my neck are standing up.

"No." She sinks down onto the couch. "I'll be all right in a moment."

"Water?" Bethy asks. At Nat's nod, she hurries out to the front entrance where we've left our bags, returning moments later with a water bottle.

"Thanks." Nat takes the water and swallows half of it. "Are you going to tell us why you made me do that? Was I right?"

Mason leans against the mantel, resting an arm along the top of it. I'd be too scared to touch it after what Nat just told us.

"No one knows for sure what happened, but you're right about the deaths. In October of 1899, someone in the house bludgeoned Philip Jr. Turner to death on this very spot. Or at least, close to it.

It happened in this room. His wife, Gracie, was killed that same night by falling against the mantel and smashing in the side of her head."

Goosebumps ripple up my arms. I refuse to look around, to make sure we're alone, or to rub the goosebumps away. I'm braver than that.

He lowers his voice. "The strange thing is, they say his sister, Caroline, who he was always very close to, was more than his sister. She was reclusive, never leaving the house, but still gave birth to two sons, Lester and Morris. The father was always unknown. The story goes that Gracie found out about Philip Jr. and Caroline and killed her husband out of disgust. Filled with rage, Caroline pushed her sister-in-law into the mantel, where she hit her head and died. Caroline was tried and hung a year later, leaving both her's and Gracie's children with no immediate family. They were sent to live with a distant relative."

"Caroline could have had an affair with a servant. I'm sure it happened all the time," I say.

From behind the camera, Conrad nods approvingly at me. "Skepticism for the win. Good. Poke holes in everything."

"Why don't we ask them?" Mason says, pulling out the spirit box.

"Oh good," Conrad says in a dry voice. "My ears will hurt."

I brace myself for some terrible noise, but it's not that bad. The sound that comes out of the spirit box is constant, but it's not painfully loud. I have to strain my ears to make out words while also listening for anything that might sneak up on us. I'll probably have a headache from it by the end of the night.

"If there's anyone with us, you can use this device to talk to us," Bethy says. She's sitting beside Nat on the couch, leaning forward, cupping her chin in her hand. I can't believe it. She almost looks bored.

Static and the occasional note of music continue to fill the room. Everyone gathers around the small box, eyes pinned on it as though that will help them decipher voices from the noise. They think this will work?

"I'm... here," a voice says through the static. It's hard to make out over the rest of the noise, but it was definitely a voice.

"I'm here. Who's here?" Conrad asks. "What's your name?"

Seconds pass.

"Gracie."

I let out a shaky breath I hadn't realized I'd been holding. It's not Caroline. Or at least whoever it is claims they're not Caroline. Good. I don't really want to commune with the ghost of a woman who would sleep with her brother. Gross.

"Did you kill your husband, Gracie?" Bethy asks.

Right, they're both murderers. But maybe Gracie's more reasonable than Caroline?

"Bad... man."

"He was a bad man because he was sleeping with his sister!" Mason shouts excitedly. "Did your husband, Philip Jr., have sex with his sister, Caroline?"

There's no answer but static.

"It was the late eighteen hundreds," I say. "I don't think she would have said it like that."

"You're right," Mason says. He frowns as he considers his words. "Gracie, did Caroline bear your husband sons?"

Long seconds filled with static pass, before the box says, *"Disgrace."*

"Did you kill him?" Conrad asks.

"No choice."

"She killed him because she had no choice. He was being disgraceful." Mason dances from foot to foot, barely able to contain himself. "I can't believe the answers we're getting."

"I know, right?" Bethy leans forward, her eyes gleaming in the darkness. "Did Caroline kill you?"

Another voice comes through the spirit box, different from the one before. I lean forward, but the words are inaudible, just a continuous, angry tone. It's deep, like a man's voice. Gracie speaks again. *"Please."*

"Please what?" Bethy asks. "Do you need help?"

Glass crashes against the floor. Mason squeals, skittering away from the mantel, as Conrad spins towards the noise. Without realizing it, I've darted towards the door, away from the commotion. I move cautiously back to stand behind the couch, with Nat and Bethy.

"The vase," Conrad says, numbly. "It shattered."

The vase of roses, once on the mantel, is now in a hundred pieces on the hardwood floor. A pool of water spreads out from under the stems of roses. The shattered glass and water gleam in the light from the camera.

"Let's take a break and clean that up. Will the Lees believe us if we say it was the ghost?" Nat asks.

Mason nods, still staring at the shattered vase. "They said things fall off counters and move by themselves all the time. I just didn't think we'd actually see it."

"Can we turn on the lights for a while?" Nat asks. "It isn't safe with all this broken glass."

I'm the closest to the light switch, so I feel my way to the wall and squeeze my eyes shut. "Lights are coming on!"

"We've got so much proof. I can't believe it." Bethy's still focused on the activity in the house. "Like the door? It moved on its own. We saw that."

Mason is blinking in the light. He runs a hand through his hair. "That's different, though. There could be a draft or the floor could be uneven. There's no good way to make this"— he gestures at the shattered glass—"believable."

"I thought you were a believer, but now you sound like me," Conrad says. "You talk big most of the time."

"I guess I'm not so sure."

"While you debate this, I'll find a broom," Nat sighs.

"I'll help," Bethy says, powering off the spirit box. "I need a breather."

Conrad sets down the camera. "I need a smoke."

"Really?" Bethy whines. "You know they'll kill you."

He turns and gives her a gesture I can't see. She chuckles.

"Can I join you?" I ask him. "I could use a smoke tonight."

"You smoke?" Mason spins on me. "You don't look like a smoker."

"The more the merrier," Conrad says, putting an arm around my shoulder and leading me out of the room.

Chapter Five

"I'll have to bum one, if that's okay," I say, when we're outside.

Conrad pulls a pack of smokes from his jacket pocket and offers me one. He lights mine before he lights his, like an old-fashioned gentleman. "Mason's right. You don't look like a smoker. Too pristine."

"Are you an ninja? You look like you've killed things."

He stares at me for a moment before grinning. "Touché."

It's dark out here, with only a bit of light coming from the streetlight at the end of the driveway. We're leaning against the side of the house, well away from the front door. The wind has picked up. Around us, the trees groan with the force of it, their leaves rustling loudly. The air, which had already been cool, is now frigid and damp. I might not have dressed warm enough. Thankfully, we'll mostly be in the house. Too bad it's haunted.

"To be fair," I say, looking at the cigarette between my fingers. "I only smoke occasionally. I haven't smoked for over a year."

Not since before Riley...

I inhale the hot smoke. It burns against the back of my throat and fills my lungs. I know it's bad for me, but I immediately feel more relaxed, despite the memories it brings back. Riley was the smoker. I only did it because she did. But now, it's something to take my mind off the ghosts inside the house and the fact that Riley's been strangely absent since we started the ghost hunt. That makes me hope she's just a figment of my imagination. If she was real, she could have come through at any point. I must have been so busy looking for real ghosts that I haven't had the energy to imagine the one haunting me. That's a relief, except... I'm pretty sure Nat saw her outside before we began.

Conrad lets out a lungful of smoke slowly, clearly relishing the act, like Riley used to.

"I told Bethy I'd quit," he says. "But these ghosts hunts make me want one every time."

"Don't tell me you're chicken. Are you the secret believer and Mason's the skeptic?"

He laughs. I think it's the first time I've heard him do that. It's nice. He's kind of intimidating, but I think he's probably a fun guy under that stern exterior.

"I don't think I believe, but you've got to admit some things we've seen tonight are unsettling."

"How'd you get into ghost hunting if you're such a skeptic?" I ask, kicking at a leaf on the ground. The wind picks it up and skitters it away.

"Mason and I have been friends for years. He was that annoying only child with no other boys his age on the block, so sometimes he hung around with me and my friends. Once he got to college, he wanted to start ghost hunting, but was too scared to go alone. Plus, he needed someone with steady hands to hold the camera. He wanted to document proof." The end of Conrad's cigarette glows orange in the darkness. There's just enough light from the street-lamps down the driveway to highlight the planes of his face. "Bethy was his best friend, and somehow this whole thing became... well, a thing. I'm a ghost hunter."

I inhale more smoke, enjoying the tendrils that leak out through my nostrils like I'm a dragon.

"What about you?" he asks, without looking at me. "What's your story?"

I shrug. "Not much to tell."

"You sure?" His voice doesn't change. I can't see him well enough to read his expression; just puffs of smoke as he speaks. "To me, it looks like you're living out of your car."

"What's wrong with that?" There's a defensive tone to my voice. I soften it. "I'm not ready to go to college or plan out the rest of my life. I'm a free spirit."

My voice cracks on the last two words, belying my claim.

Our smoky exhales combine, white against the black of the night sky, before a gust of wind blows them downhill.

"I looked you up on social media," he says, nonchalant as ever. "You don't exist."

"I don't think much of putting my life up online for everyone to see." My heart rate picks up. I toss the rest of my cigarette to the driveway and crush it under the toe of my runner.

"Funny thing," he continues, as though I hadn't said anything. "There was a profile for Riley Miller. She seemed like a bright kid. Died suddenly last year."

My stomach drops, but he doesn't stop.

"There was a girl that looked a lot like you in most of her pictures. She was tagged too. Know anything about that, Lanie Gilbert?"

Slowly, I slide down the wall, until I'm crouched against it, my hair falling over my face to hide me from the night. Familiar pain shoots through my chest, like razor blades slicing my heart. I can't breathe.

"Are you okay?" Conrad asks, sinking to the ground beside me.

I don't answer. I can't. My fingers smell like smoke as I rub my eyes. My throat is tight with the pressure of unshed tears. I shake my head—no, I'm not okay. I'm beyond help. There's a squeezing pressure on my chest, like I haven't lost enough and it's going to take my life, too. Suddenly, the dam breaks and I'm hugging my knees, sobbing into the denim of my jeans, feeling more lost and alone than I have since I first realized Riley was gone.

"Hey." Conrad tosses his cigarette into the drive, then wraps his arms around me and pulls me in to his side so I'm leaning awkwardly against him. It only makes me sob harder while I cling to his jacket. I can't stop. The tears keep flowing, and my nose is plugged but streaming, all at once. It makes no sense, this physical reaction, my emotions. It's been a *year*!

Conrad pats my back and says nothing until I take a shuddering breath. Then, he says, "You don't have to tell me. I'll keep your secret, but if you need to talk about it, you can talk to me."

"What's taking so long?" Mason calls out the front door. "Are you smoking the whole pack? Come on!"

I let go of Conrad's jacket. There's a wet patch on the denim. I brush at it, hoping he's not covered in my snot. He pulls a tissue out of his pocket.

"It's a little linty."

"Thanks." I hiccup and blow my nose. The tissue is linty and a bit gritty. My eyes are scratchy and probably bright red, but I take a deep, cleansing breath.

"You're not in trouble, are you?"

We're sitting so close our thighs are touching. I scoot over an inch, the air unbearably cold in the new distance between us. "No. I guess I'm a runaway, but I'm eighteen, so not even technically that."

"You know how to get ahold of me if you need anything." He rolls athletically to his feet. I bet he took some sort of martial arts as a kid. I wouldn't have guessed he was a smoker either.

"I have your number," I say.

He extends a hand to help me up. "Are you okay to go in or do you need more time? Mason can wait."

I shake my head. My brain is foggy and tired, but that's just the remnants of a hard cry. I dust driveway debris off my pants, then run fingers through my hair.

"I probably look a mess."

"You look like you've been crying, but otherwise, you look fine," he assures me.

"I'm sure Bethy loves it when you say things like that to her." I force a joking tone into my voice. It comes out as a croak. Still, I appreciate his honesty.

"It makes her very happy." His tone is dry. He opens the front door for me. "Honey, I'm home!"

I feel like he's joking to pull the attention away from me, but it doesn't work.

"Took you long enough," Mason grumbles, walking out of the living room, his phone in hand. He looks up, does a double take when he sees me, and rushes over. "What happened?"

He grabs my shoulders and moves me away from Conrad, glaring at his friend. "What did you do?"

"Nothing. She's fine." Conrad steps between us. I'm grateful. I feel closer to this taciturn man than I do Mason, who I'm pretty sure has a thing for me. "She just needs some space."

"You're sure you're all right?" Mason pushes Conrad aside so he can look me over. Nat and Bethy emerge from the living room.

"What's going on?" Bethy asks, taking me in. "Are you okay?"

"I'm fine. Nothing's wrong," I assure them. Conrad wraps an arm around Mason's shoulders and pulls him into a headlock. He drags him away from me, back into the living room. Bethy gives me an assessing look, then follows them.

"Ew, you stink like smoke," she says as she cozies in to Conrad—thankfully on his non-snotty side. I don't need her getting ideas and hating me.

Nat lingers, leaning against the wall, arms crossed.

"I'm fine," I tell her.

Her dark brown eyes are deep wells of knowledge. I feel as though she sees through me. "If you say so."

Fury sparks in my chest at her knowing tone. I tamp it down. Now is not the time to make a scene. I'd likely end up crying again. She pushes herself off the wall and saunters into the living room.

She's a stranger, I tell myself. She knows nothing about me.

Still, I'm afraid she's right. I follow her into the living room, where all the lights are still on.

"So, what's next?" I ask. "We've been in the attic and the living room. Can we conclude the place is haunted and leave?"

I want to leave, but I don't want tonight to be over. I haven't felt this much a part of something in ages. I don't know these people well, but despite our differences, they're already starting to feel like family. Or at the very least, friends. I don't even feel this way with Heather and Claire, and they're the people I've known the longest in Salvation Hills.

"Not yet. It's not even midnight." Mason hands Conrad the camera. "We could continue in here, but I think it would be good to try another part of the house."

He pauses for dramatic effect.

Conrad rolls his eyes and sighs. "Where?"

"The kitchen." Mason points to the back of the house, then leads us there like a tour guide, flicking off lights as he goes.

"Why?" Nat's tone is suspicious. "You're going to make me sense things again, aren't you?"

"That *is* why you're here."

The kitchen is the same mix of modern and antique furnishings as the rest of the house. The hardwood floors are shined to a polish, reflecting the light of our camera. There's an island in the centre of the room, outfitted with a dishwasher that certainly isn't original to the house. The countertops are quartz, the appliances chrome. The cupboards, which could very well be original, are painted a fresh white. Copper pots hang from the ceiling. Everything is so shiny, which is weird when we only have one light. Despite the darkness, there seems to be light radiating through the room.

Large windows look out over the big backyard. Outside is pitch black, no lights beyond us, no signs of life. If we needed to run for help, I wouldn't know where to go. Across the expanse of night-blackened grass, the trees encroach on the property, their branches swaying in the wind.

We settle around the island with Conrad a step back from the rest of us, camera ready.

"Give it your best," Mason tells Nat, rubbing his hands together like a millionaire at the bank. He's so eager.

Bethy pulls out a barstool and leans against the island. She plays with the ends of her ponytail. I stand beside her, bracing my hip against the countertop.

Nat shifts from foot to foot, eyes closed, rocking slightly. Her hands are clasped under her chin. Her brow creases with concentration, then smooths as she speaks. "I see two men, living together. They love each other, but platonically. I want to say... they're brothers?"

Mason lets out a giddy laugh, then claps a hand over his mouth.

Nat flinches. "There's fire. It started in here. I don't know how." She opens her eyes. "At least one of them died in the fire."

"Oh my god!" Mason says. "Everything's right. Did you get a sense of the time period?"

Nat pulls herself up so she's sitting on the counter, swinging her legs like a child. "It was a while ago, but decades, not centuries."

"That's awesome." Mason is almost dancing with excitement. "Two families lived here after the deaths of Philip Jr., Gracie and Caroline. In 1920, after the last family moved out, Lester Turner, now an adult, bought the house and moved in with his brother, Morris."

"Lester and Morris? Are these the kids the brother and sister supposedly had together?" Bethy asks, her voice thick with disgust. "The inbred ones?"

"Yes."

"Cool. And gross."

Mason rolls his eyes theatrically. "Can I continue?"

Bethy nods, so Mason does, referencing the notes on his phone. "A fire broke out in 1942. It started in the kitchen. Morris, the younger of the two brothers, died in it."

"Is he here?" I ask.

Nat shrugs, her dark curls bobbing about her shoulders. "There are a lot of spirits here, but they're hiding from me."

"Should we try to communicate with them?" Bethy asks.

The pots hanging above the island rattle. We all look up. I take a step back.

"Wind," Conrad says, holding the camera up to catch the moving pots. "It's probably the wind."

"The wind's been blowing like this all evening. Plus, there's no draft," Mason says. "We know there's no one upstairs, so it can't be movement through the house."

"Yeah, it could be," Bethy says. "There could be a ghost up there."

"Let's split up then," Mason says. "We'll each take a camera and go to different parts of the house. I call dibs on Riley!"

I cross my arms over my chest. "You don't get to call dibs on me. I'm a person."

"Well then, who do you want to go with?" He leans forward, waiting for my answer. I shift, suddenly anxious.

"Me." Nat jumps off the counter and rounds the island to put her arm around me.

"Sure." I try not to flinch away from her or lean into her touch. I'm finding tonight's sudden physical contact jarring. I've been alone for a year; I don't know how to act anymore.

"Then who am I going with?" Mason whines. "Obviously, Conrad and Bethy are going together."

"Obviously," Conrad agrees.

"Maybe you should make better friends." Bethy hops off her stool, taking Conrad's hand. "We call *dibs* on the second floor!"

"First floor!" Mason yells before I've even realized we're claiming our search areas. He points at me and Nat and says in a sing-song voice, "You get the attic!"

My stomach twists, but Nat's arm is steady and warm around my shoulders, reminding me that I'm not alone in this.

I nod. "Great. The attic."

· · · · · · · · · ·

A few minutes later, I open the door at the end of the second-floor hallway. It's hard to find in the dark unless you know it's there, but I bet when it was built it blended in so well that the family couldn't see where the servants—or slaves—disappeared to after taking care of their needs. I aim the handheld camera at the dark hole beyond the open door.

"Ready?" Nat asks, her hand on the small of my back. "Want me to go first?"

I don't know if it's worse to go first or last, so I shake my head and step into the steep, narrow stairwell. I take the steps cautiously. At the top of the stairs, a small window looks out over the yard. I can see nothing but trees and their tossing branches.

When the house was built, a person could probably see the whole farm, including any outbuildings, from this window. Who would have looked out here, hoping to catch sight of their family? Sadness tightens my chest. I take a deep breath and step out into the room. It's cooler than before, more bearable than a few hours ago, though the wind roaring through the trees and whistling around the house makes it hard to hear anything. I strain my ears for any out-of-place thuds or creaks.

Nat walks past me and sits down cross-legged on the dusty floor near the centre of the room. She sets something on the floor. Light flares. As I come closer, I realize she's lit a tea light.

"Do you normally carry candles in your pockets?" I ask, standing beside her.

"I do on investigations." She pats the floor. "Come sit."

I set the camera on the floor, double checking that we'll both be in the shot, then sit across from her. I feel the dark space of the attic loom behind me. I glance over my shoulder. Nothing's there. Outside, there's a rush of air, then the patter of raindrops on the roof. The scent of rain and soaked earth quickly permeates the attic.

Nat rummages in her pocket and pulls out a flask. The scent of whiskey spreads through the room as Nat pours it into a shot glass next to the candle. She places an open packet of raisins and a flashing ball next to it. The ball goes dark after a few seconds of stillness.

"Dried fruit was more special when they were alive than it is now," she says, seeing my quizzical look. "Plus, it's easy to carry." She doesn't explain the ball.

"What are you doing?"

"Offering them food and drink. It might encourage them to show themselves to us."

I shiver. Hopefully not to me. Though, being up here with Nat is more peaceful than when we were all here. She brings a calming presence, something I'd like to learn to replicate. Still, I feel uneasy.

"I know your life was hard," she says to the empty room. "You weren't treated well. I've brought you some food and drink. You're welcome to it. It's for you."

The candle lights up the planes of her face, making her ethereally beautiful, almost spookily so. She looks up and catches me watching her. I glance quickly down at the food, waiting to see it move, or *do* something.

The atmosphere of the room has changed. The darkness behind me is still uncomfortable, but the fear I felt from it has lessened. It's *almost* peaceful.

Nat draws in a quick breath, but her voice is calm when she asks, "Do you feel that?"

"What?" I look around, but I'm not afraid.

"Look at the whiskey. Can you sense anything?"

I gaze at it until my vision begins to unfocus. Only then do I see it: a nuclear green mist rising from the shot glass and box of raisins to the space between Nat and me. "What is it?"

"A spirit, taking the energy from our offerings. You can't see her?"

I shake my head. The way Nat's talking, I want to see her. Kind of.

"A Black girl, about your age, maybe younger, with her hair tightly up, wearing a plain dress." Nat doesn't move while she describes the ghost, just looks sidelong in the direction of the green mist, which is now floating up and over into the space beside us. When I try to focus, the green mist disappears. I allow my eyes to unfocus again. This time the mist becomes visible faster.

Nat moves the ball closer to the ghost. It twinkles in her hand, the lights turning off when she sets it down. A cat toy. "Can you touch this?" Nat asks the ghost. "Make it move?"

I wish I could see the ghost, hear her. Ask questions that need more substantial answers than a yes or a no. I'm tired of asking *Please make this move.* There's no satisfaction to that.

The ball sparkles, rolling half an inch.

"Who are you?"

There's a rush of wind, a thunderous pattering on the roof above us. I jump, gasping.

"It's just rain," Nat says in a calm monotone, not looking at me.

"Sorry." I rub my hands on my jeans, clear my throat. "Did you get a name?"

"No. She's gone now. The spirits here are strangely skittish, but someone is active. Bethy was touched and doors have slammed."

"Don't forget the vase," I remind her.

"Of course. I've been seeing something else, as well. It's out of reach." She ponders this, then asks, "What about you?"

"What about me?" I ask.

"Have you been sensing anything?"

"What? No, nothing. Why?" *Act normal,* I tell myself. She doesn't *know* I'm haunted. Because I'm not. I can't be. "All I know is you couldn't pay me to live in this house."

"I think everyone's sensitive to a degree, but you more than most. You could have abilities. The gift." She picks up the items, and blows out the candle. Darkness closes around us, but it's not as frightening as before. "Did you know there's a spirit attached to you? A teenage girl with short, black hair?"

"No. There's not." I dart to my feet, heading for the stairs. She's wrong. She has to be wrong. Riley has not been trapped with me this past year. She moved on and is enjoying whatever the afterlife offers. Guilt consumes me, makes my hands shake. I'm crazy, that's all. I am *not* haunted.

"It's not Riley, is it?" Nat asks in a soft voice. "Your name?"

I'm at the top of the stairs. I spin to face her.

"You know nothing about me." The anger in my voice makes it sound like a stranger's.

"What are you running from?" she asks calmly. I glance at the camera she's picked up, but the light is off. "I'm not recording."

"I'm not running from anything." I turn to head down the stairs.

"Yes, you are." Riley appears beside me, her eyebrows quirked and mouth in a frown. She takes a step towards me. *"Just admit it. You'll feel much better."*

An invisible force hits my shoulder. My arms windmill as I try to catch my balance. The staircase is dark, looming below me.

I scream as I fall towards it.

Chapter Six

"Riley!" Nat screams. She grabs for my hand. My fingers glide across her palm, and I'm sure she's too late—but then her fingers clasp mine and she yanks me away from the black pit of the stairwell. We land on the floor with a loud crash that shakes the house.

Shouts and footsteps echo from the second floor below.

"Ow." I sit up, rubbing my throbbing elbow. My hip and knee hurt too. "Thanks."

"Did she push you?" Nat asks.

I look around. Riley is gone. "No. She didn't push me. Something else did. You saw her?"

"I told you. She's been hanging around you all night." Nat sits up, rubbing the side she landed on.

I shake my head, hot, terrified tears running down my cheeks. I sit up and brush them away as the door to the stairwell opens, letting in bright light. Conrad fumbles against the wall until he finds the switch. The naked bulbs hanging from the attic ceiling cast bobbing shadows as they sway in a draft.

"What happened? Are you guys okay?" he asks, hurrying up the stairs, followed by a pale, wide-eyed Bethy. Her purple hair is falling out of her ponytail into her face. Mason's agitated voice shouts from downstairs, demanding to know what's going on. Nat gives me an assessing look.

I find my spare elastic on my wrist and pull my hair into a messy ponytail. "I'm fine. Something almost pushed me down the stairs."

Conrad shines the light in my face, then Nat's, as though evaluating our truthfulness.

Nat nods. "I barely caught her hand before she took a nosedive."

"Did you get it on camera?" Bethy asks.

I'd forgotten about the camera, as had Nat, judging by her expression. She grabs it from the floor where it landed and turns it over in her hands, powering it on. It works. She gives a sigh of relief. "It's fine, but it wasn't recording."

"Mason won't like that," Bethy says.

"Mason can suck it up." Conrad's face darkens. "We can't catch every supernatural moment on camera. Besides, Riley almost died just now."

I almost died? That's pretty dramatic but he could be right. The stairs are steep and I almost took a header. My stomach roils with nausea. Any peace I felt up here is now long gone. I sink down until I'm sitting on the floor. Standing in front of the stairs doesn't seem like a good idea.

"What's going on, you guys?" Mason asks, poking his head in the door. "I thought we were splitting up. I've been investigating the creepy first floor on my own, you know."

"Riley almost died," Bethy tells him, deadpan.

"What? Are you okay?" He pushes past Bethy and Conrad and sits on the top step beside me. I'm momentarily touched that he cares that much about me—until he grabs the camera from Nat and turns on the replay. "Did you catch it on camera?"

"Told you," Bethy says, as she flicks purple hair out of her face. "It's always about the footage."

"No, we didn't catch it on camera." Nat's voice is sharp. "We were having a private conversation that I wasn't inclined to film."

"About what?" Mason doesn't look at her, instead going over the last minutes of our footage.

"It was private," Nat retorts. She climbs to her feet with a groan.

"Come *on*. We're here to prove that ghosts are real, not have girl talk in the attic. Obviously, you pissed off the ghost, so you may as well share." He passes the camera back to Nat, who heaves an impressive sigh.

"Fine. Riley—"

"No. Don't tell them," I beg, grabbing her sleeve. I can't believe her—

She shakes me loose. "Riley's a sensitive. She can sense things better than most. I was about to encourage her to work on that gift when she was pushed."

My burst of anger evaporates. I'd thought Nat was going to share my secret. She didn't, so maybe I can trust her. I'm still not going to spill my guts, though. I barely know her.

"Hey, that's good!" Mason pulls me against him in an energetic hug, squeezing and shaking me. I inch out of his hold. "We're having fun with you, so you should come to more ghost hunts."

I'm not sure I want to. It's been fun, but it's also been terrifying, with more tears than I'd like. The camaraderie is nice, though.

"Maybe your presence, as a medium and a sensitive, is why this place is so active," Mason says.

"I don't think so," Nat says. "This place isn't welcoming."

"Can we leave the creepy attic?" Bethy asks. She doesn't wait for an answer. She's closest to the door, and she ducks out, followed by Conrad.

"Yeah, I don't want to be up here." I stand. Mason takes my arm as though I'm likely to take another tumble. I don't shake him off.

Moments later, we're on the second floor with the door to the attic firmly closed and latched.

"So, you didn't get the push, but what *did* you get on camera?" Mason asks.

"Everything until we got up to leave," Nat says. "I offered some food and drink. A young woman appeared, in period clothing. A slave or servant, but she said nothing. The rain started, and she disappeared. How about you?"

"Not much," Bethy says. "We heard footsteps, and the flashlights turned on, but nothing conclusive."

"The footsteps could have been you guys," Conrad says to Nat and me.

"What about you, Mase?" Nat asks.

Mason grins. "I thought of something while you were upstairs. The cellar is probably original to the house. Mr. Lee told me we have to go outside to access it. But..."

The camera light illuminates Mason's face from below, like when kids tell ghost stories around the campfire, making him look frightening and inhuman. "I went around outside and found the cellar. It's padlocked, but I texted Mr. Lee. He told me where the key was and warned me to be careful because it's a small, old space." Mason holds up the key between his thumb and index finger. "Guess where we're going next?"

I cross my arms tightly over my chest while Bethy coos with excitement. I don't want to go there. An ancient, haunted cellar in a storm sounds terrifying. After the incident in the attic, I'm not looking forward to it.

"Get your coats if you want them," Mason yells, running down the main staircase. "It's raining!"

· · · ● · ● · · · ·

Nat catches my elbow as Conrad and Bethy follow an eager Mason out of the house. "Are you okay after all that?"

Oh no. I hope she isn't starting this again. I yank my arm away. "I'm fine. Can we please not talk about it?"

Nat holds up her hands in mock surrender. "You're the one being haunted."

Outside, the rain pelts me with large, cold drops. It isn't coming down too hard, and as soon as I round the corner, the roof overhang protects me from it. I nearly run into Bethy and Conrad in the darkness. They're huddled next to the wooden cellar doors Mason is trying to unlock. He fumbles with the padlock, fighting the wind and rain.

"It's not opening!"

"Let's go back inside then," Conrad yells, motioning for Bethy, Nat and me to turn around. As I do, my eye catches on a shadow beneath the trees. It's a man, silhouetted against the navy skyline, half hidden by the swaying branches. I freeze, my limbs going weak and heavy with fear. It's dark, but it couldn't be clearer: the still figure of a man amongst the thrashing branches. There's no way it's my imagination.

Bethy screams, lifting her finger to point at the trees. Her eyes are pinned to the same spot I'd been staring at. When I look back, the man is gone.

"What?" Conrad spins around, training the light of the camera on the trees. There's nothing there, just a tangle of underbrush and thrashing branches.

"There was a man. There was one hundred percent a man standing there." Her hand shakes as she points beneath the swaying boughs. "He's gone, but he was standing right there."

Conrad takes a few steps forward, towards the dark barrier of the trees. Bethy shrieks and grabs his sleeve. "Don't go. What if he gets you?"

"Do you think this was a real man or a ghost? That underbrush is pretty thick."

Bethy shrugs, huddling close to Conrad. "I don't know. He disappeared so fast. Maybe it was a ghost, but I could have sworn he was real. I don't see ghosts."

"Do you sense anything, Nat?" Mason asks. His face is ashen, his auburn hair dark with rain and stuck to his forehead.

"Nothing," Nat says. "Riley?"

All I feel is afraid. I hug myself tightly, scanning the shadows under the trees. They seem to move on their own, as though alive with their own consciousness. "It looked like a real man."

"You saw it too?" Bethy asks, half turning to me, though she keeps herself pressed into Conrad's side.

"What did he look like?" Mason takes a short step towards the trees, then shuffles towards us.

"Can we go inside and talk about this?" Nat asks. "If he's a physical man... We left the door unlocked."

A chill runs through me, but I don't run for the door. Instead, I hang back, letting Conrad lead the way, then fall in beside Nat. There is no way I'm hanging out on the edge of the group. Mason takes up the rear. I scan the property again, my eyes straining against the darkness and shifting shadows. I catch Mason doing the same thing. His fear doesn't make me feel better.

Our steps echo hollowly across the verandah, but the house is quiet when we step inside. Not quiet in a comfortable way. Quiet in a something-could-happen-at-any-moment way. The darkness doesn't help. When Mason locks the door, the click of the lock echoes through the entryway, ominous. I slump onto the bench over a built-in boot rack. I'm drained and just want this night to be over.

Everyone looks at Bethy and me.

"So? Was he a real man?" Conrad asks.

Bethy laughs. It's a shrill sound, devoid of humour. "How could he be real? The weather is ridiculous. He has to have been a ghost."

"But you saw him. You're not sensitive, are you?" Conrad takes Bethy's hands and rubs them between his own. I look away. It's such a sweet gesture, so intimate. It makes me want someone who would do the same for me. But I don't think I can care for someone that much. What happens when they leave me? I squeeze my arms tighter around myself.

"Maybe it was a neighbour coming to check out the screaming?" Mason asks.

"A neighbour would have brought a light. I would have, at least," Bethy says. "You could use it to blind the intruders or bash them over the head."

Conrad chuckles at Bethy, but shakes his head. "This property is huge, and over the storm? There's no way anyone heard us. We're at the very end of the road. The rest of the houses are way off. These yards are gigantic."

That isn't a comforting thought, that we're so isolated out here. I want to call it a night, but I don't want to be the one to say it. Before, when I suggested it, they all turned me down. I'm physically tired and emotionally drained. I just want a safe place to sleep, but I'm stuck here until someone else chickens out first. I can't say I'm looking forward to sleeping in my car after tonight's frights, either.

"If it's not a real person..." Mason says, excitement growing in his voice. He grabs my arm and shakes it in a totally non-romantic way—more like a dog with a rope toy. "Then maybe it's a ghost. How old would you say he was?"

I yank my arm away from him. "I didn't see him that well. He was in the shadows."

Bethy nods in agreement.

Mason grins, his eyes glinting in the camera's beam. "Well, we have several options. We've talked about the Turners, but there is a more recent death we haven't talked about. In 2010, this place was up for rent. No one was living here. The caretaker dropped by, noticed a bad smell and looked around. He found a backpack and clothes, but never found a body, just some rotten food. Turns out, the neighbours had reported a guy coming in and out of the house. A squatter. My guess is he died here by nefarious means."

"Nefarious means... as in...?" Bethy asks.

Mason pauses for dramatic effect. "Murder."

A chill grips me, totally unrelated to the temperature.

"But they didn't find a body. Did they find blood or anything to suggest he'd died?" Conrad asks.

"No, but he was never seen again. It has to have been murder!"

"How do you know?"

"It's a hypothesis!" Mason exclaims. "Just go with it, okay? I'm positive that's what happened."

"Okay." Conrad doesn't sound convinced. He fiddles with the camera.

"Anyway, they never found out where this guy disappeared to or who did it." Mason rubs his hands together eagerly, clearly not worried about his weak hypothesis or lack of evidence. "Maybe we will."

⋅⋅⋅●⋅●⋅⋅⋅

Mason leads us through the house to the utility room at the back. The room is fully modernized. If I'd only seen the utility room and not the rest of the house, I'd have guessed this was a brand-new home. It even smells fresh from the laundry detergent in here.

"Supposedly, they found the squatter's stuff in here. Let's see if we can get him to interact with us. Bethy, set up the flashlights."

While Bethy places the flashlights on two shelves across from each other, Mason turns on the spirit box. The static from it pulses through the room as it rapidly switches from channel to channel, drowning out the storm outside.

Bethy wiggles her way between me and Nat, positioning herself so she's in the centre of the shot, and away from any ghostly hands that might try to touch her. I'm jealous of that. The safety, not the superstar bit.

"Is there anyone here who would like to communicate with us?" Mason asks. "You can speak to us through this device or turn on the flashlights to let us know you're here. We're wanting to speak to Jason Glinsmann. Is he here?"

We stand there, silent. I barely breathe, listening for words in the static or for a light to turn on.

"Please speak to us," Bethy says.

"I'm... here."

The words are clear through the static, though I can't tell the gender of the speaker.

"Who are we speaking to? Can you tell us your name?"

"Ri—ley."

I start with a gasp. Nat reaches behind Bethy and places a calming hand on my back. Bethy glances sidelong at me.

"Why is it asking for you?" she whispers. I shake my head. I can't...

"Your name is Riley or you're here because of Riley?" Mason asks, an edge to his voice.

"Want her."

"Well, you can't have her," Mason snaps. "She doesn't belong to you. She's alive. You're not."

Conrad's dark eyes flit to me, silently assessing. He and Nat are the only ones who know the truth.

For a second, I'm relieved. It can't be Riley's ghost speaking if they want me. Or her. But then the creepiness hits me. Then who is this? And what do they want from us? From me? Why do they want Riley?

My chest tightens. I think I'm going to be sick. I put Riley at risk by coming here. Are they trying to catch her spirit? Or is it me they want? Something tried to kill me. Maybe it is me they're after, after all. I shake off my uneasiness, letting my anger in.

"Who are you?" I demand.

Unintelligible static fills the air.

"How many of you are there?" Mason furrows his brow.

"Seven."

"Okay, seven of you." Mason leans towards the spirit box. "Did you die here?"

"We came."

A crack of lightning flashes in the window above the washing machine, momentarily blinding me. Bethy squeaks. The following crash of thunder shakes the house. In the silence that follows, Mason looks around at us, "They came? What does that mean?"

To the room, he says, "Are you ghosts?"

No answer, just static.

"How did you come here?"

Again, static fills the room.

Suddenly, both flashlights blink on. Mason screams, making me jump. I shield my eyes with my hand, adrenaline pumping through my veins. My heart is beating so hard, it feels like it'll break my ribs.

"Oh," Bethy says, breathless. "That was scary."

The spirit box crackles.

"Leave. Now." The voice that comes through the radio is firm, almost angry. *"Get out."*

"What?" Mason asks. "Why do you want us to leave? Don't you want us to tell your story?"

A chill settles on me, like the gush of cold air that comes out of the freezer. I rub my arms, looking for the source. The window is closed and the vents are off. The oppressiveness of those words settles like a hand pressing against my chest. It almost hurts. I rub at my collarbone to ease it.

"It's freezing," Conrad says. "Is it the AC?"

"No," Nat says. "It's too cold outside for AC."

"The vent's off," I say, holding my hand in front of it. "Nothing."

"I think we should leave," Nat says. "Leave this room at least."

There's something off about her voice. She sounds strained.

"But we're just getting started," Mason whines.

"Let's go." I reach across Bethy and take Nat's hand to lead her through the circle we'd created with our bodies, and out into the hall. None of the rooms in this house feel safe. There's a presence here that raises the hairs on the back of my neck. I don't like any of it. I don't want to be here, but I help Nat to the living room and onto the couch. "What happened? Are you all right?"

She shakes her head, massaging her temples. "Didn't you feel it? The oppressive need to get out?"

I shrug. "I was scared. That's all."

She taps two fingers against the centre of my collarbone, right against the spot I'd been massaging in the utility room. Without me noticing, the tension there has gone.

"We have some work to do, you and I," she says. "But I don't think we'll start here. No sense pulling down your shields when you might need them."

"What do you mean? What shields?" I don't know what she's talking about. Before tonight, I hadn't believed in ghosts, had thought I was crazy. I'm still not sure about being a sensitive.

"You're protecting yourself without realizing it. It's subconscious. You can sense them, the spirits, but you're not letting them get through to you. It's not a bad thing. It's good. A natural barrier you've created. Be careful not to let them get through unless you want them to. They could wreak havoc on you." She lifts her hand and brushes a strand of my hair behind my ear. I shake my head and pull away.

"What about..." I hesitate to voice what we had talked about earlier—that I'm being haunted by my ghost best friend. Mason, Conrad and Bethy's voices are getting closer. I don't want them to hear this.

"Your ghost?" Nat leans back against the couch cushions, sighing as though in pain. She rubs her temples. "I think you let her through subconsciously, but aren't ready to deal with her. That's the first thing you'll have to do."

Deal with her. That sounds rough. Sick. What if I don't want to deal with her? But Nat's right. Riley shouldn't be stuck here with me. That's why I'd convinced myself she wasn't real.

Mason enters the room first. He snaps his fingers at us. "What are we doing? Having a picnic instead of ghost hunting? The Lees didn't let us into their house to lounge around. Let's go."

"Seriously, Mason," Bethy says. "Cool it."

"Yeah," I add, suddenly annoyed with Mason. He is so oblivious. "Clearly, Nat isn't feeling well."

"Oh, really?" He rushes to the couch and leans over the back, all concern now. "What happened? Did you sense something?"

Nat waves her hand at him. "I'm fine. Just give me a second. What do you want to investigate next?"

"What time is it?" Mason asks.

Conrad checks the clock on his phone. "Nearly one o'clock."

"Perfect. I know just what we'll do next."

CHAPTER SEVEN

Eric Lee's bedroom looks like any ordinary boy's room, except it's clean and organized. No toys are on the floor and the books in the bookcase are organized largest to smallest. I'm sure the Lees made their children clean their rooms before we came. I don't know a kid his age that actually picks up after themselves. There's a quilt on the bed, the corners tucked in. Sports and gaming posters hang on the blue walls, and a football sits on the edge of the desk beside a laptop. I didn't get a laptop until I was sixteen. I'm surprised he left it when they went on their trip. Maybe, like my parents, Mr. and Mrs. Lee had forbidden technology in favour of "quality family time." Maybe they actually have quality family time; I'm still not sure what that is.

The exterior wall has two large windows on either side of the bed, framed with sheer curtains. Beyond them, the storm is gathering force, and tree branches thrash in the wind. The yard beneath the trees is too dark for me to tell if someone is lurking under them.

The thought that we might be visible to someone below makes my skin crawl. I can't seem to look away from the dark glass.

"This is Eric's room," Mason says. "Mrs. Lee says it's one of the most active rooms in the house. Eric's okay to be in it during the day, but often sleeps on his sister's floor because he's scared to be alone in here at night."

"That's awful," Bethy murmurs. "But what can we do about it?"

"I'm hoping Nat can tell who's here," Mason says, his gaze on the medium, expectant.

Nat sways beside me. I place a hand on her back to steady her, but she shakes her head, indicating she's just sensing the room. "They see things in here. Full body apparitions?"

Mason nods vigorously. "Yeah. I'm thinking it's Lester. He lived here until he was too old to take care of himself. According to stories he told staff at the care home, this was his mother Caroline's room. I think we should reach out to her."

A sudden chill comes over me. I glance quickly over my shoulder, but the darkened doorway and the hallway beyond are empty. Nat raises her eyebrows.

"Just a creepy-crawly feeling," I assure her.

"Pay attention to that," she tells me.

Mason pulls a flashing cat ball from his pocket and places it on the floor, while Bethy sets the two flashlights on either side of the room. The static of the spirit box fills the air, making me jump. I wasn't ready for it to be turned on.

"Caroline, if you're here, we'd like to talk to you," Mason says. "Can you give us a sign of your presence? You could turn on these devices or speak to us if you'd like."

Several long seconds pass with no answer. I look at the others, but they're focused on the box.

"There's at least one spirit here," Nat says, staring forward dreamily. "I can feel it, but I can't tell its gender."

"Caroline, if that's you, speak to us through this box," Mason says sternly.

The wind moans around the house, rattling the windowpanes.

A staticky, almost inaudible, voice emanates from the box. *"Alone... dark."*

It doesn't sound like a woman to me.

"Are you alone in the dark?" Mason asks, intent on the disembodied voice. When there is no immediate answer, he continues. "Are you Caroline? Was this your room?"

"I am... here," the voice says.

"Does that mean it's her?" Bethy asks. Louder, she says, "Is this Caroline we're speaking to?"

"Caroline, were you having an affair with your brother, Philip Jr.?"

"He's here."

The voice is low, sing-song. My chest tightens. My palms are clammy and dread courses through me. Mason and Bethy look at each other wide-eyed, excited. I don't think it's Caroline we're talking to. There's something off about the voice, but I can't quite tell what it is. They're putting an awful lot of trust in the spirit to tell the truth. Most living humans I know aren't that honest. Why would spirits be any different?

"Is that a yes?" Mason asks the voice. "Why would you have an affair with your brother?"

A deafening clatter reverberates through the floor. I startle, gasping. Nat runs her thumb over the back of my hand. I must have grabbed her in my fear. I loosen my death grip on her hand, but don't let go. A dull, rhythmic thudding continues, barely audible over the patter of rain on the glass, though the clattering is gone.

"What was that?" Bethy asks. She's standing beside Conrad, holding his hand in a white-knuckled grip. I'm not the only one clinging on to someone else for comfort. Mason, again, is the odd man out.

He takes a tentative step to the window, where the thudding sound is coming from. He swallows audibly as he peers out. "I don't see anything."

"It sounded like it came from outside, but it isn't thunder. More like something came loose." Conrad stays beside Bethy. He can't move with the grip she's got on him. "Should we go investigate?"

The look Mason gives him seems to say *No way in hell*, but he nods. "Ladies first."

Nat smirks, shaking her head at Mason, but leads the way, which means I lead the way at her side, my hand still clamped in hers. I keep my head up, eyes forward, though I want to peer down each side of the dark hallway and swivel my head to peek around the banister before we start down the stairs. *Conrad has a camera on you,* I remind myself. I've probably made a fool out of myself tonight, but I don't want to look like a complete idiot in the video.

When we reach the main floor, Nat leads us into the kitchen rather than towards the front door. The thudding continues.

Whump, whump, whump.

The kitchen is at the back of the house, underneath Eric—and Caroline's—room. It leads out to a mudroom. Outside, the rain has picked up, coming down in sheets of water. When we step out onto the porch, I realize Nat's trying to keep us from getting drenched. The thudding continues, louder now that we're downstairs.

The porch is a small room. To the left is a door with steps leading to the back lawn. On the wall opposite the door is a boot rack with coat hooks above it. The floor is covered with that old, super thin carpet that doesn't do much of anything except look ugly. I bet it dates back to the sixties. I'm surprised it hasn't been replaced yet. Each wall is windowed, equipped with raised venetian blinds. The glass is dusty, water-streaked. Between the dirty windows, the rain, and the darkness, it's almost impossible to see outside.

I rub the glass, trying to see past the water streaming down the pane. The sound is coming from back here, but I can't tell from where. Mason pushes past Nat and me to peer out the window himself.

"Is that...?"

He unlocks the back door and steps into the downpour, his clothes darkening with water. The sound crescendos, less rhythmic than I had first thought, dull thuds broken by a low creak.

He walks to the edge of the house and peers around the corner. Conrad aims the camera after him. None of us follow him into the rain. When he turns back to us, his hair is stuck to his scalp. His skin is pale and washed out from the faint camera light, and he blinks against the droplets pelting his face. He shouts to be heard over the storm. "It's the cellar door!"

"I thought it was locked," Bethy says in a small voice, hugging herself with her arms. She looks up at Conrad. "I don't want to go out there."

"I think we've got to." He takes a deep breath, shakes his head as though to clear it, and steps out into the storm.

Bethy glances at Nat and me, wild-eyed, but follows a step behind her boyfriend. Conrad is rushing to catch up with Mason, who's already disappeared around the corner of the house.

I turn to Nat. "I thought the cellar was padlocked. How is it open?"

She shrugs. "I don't know. The spirits maybe? If they want us down there, they'll find a way."

Terrible thought. Why would they want us in the cellar? It can't be for anything good. "Is Mason the kind of guy who would get someone to come open it just to scare us? For the video content?"

She considers this. "Maybe for a joke, but not for something like this. He honestly wants to believe and catch some sort of evidence. I've known him for a few years and he's done nothing like that before."

My last shred of hope, the one that was chanting *everything's going to be all right,* dies inside me. I don't want to go out there or into the cellar. But I've committed to this, and I don't want to be left behind in the creepy house while everyone else investigates.

Nat holds out her hand. I grip it tightly and follow her out into the darkness, pausing to close the porch door behind us. When we catch up to the others, Mason is standing at the mouth of the open cellar. Darkness, somehow darker than the night surrounding us, looms before him. Bethy stares at it, wide-eyed and still. She looks as horrified as I feel.

"Ready?" Mason shouts over the rush of wind and hammering rain. His voice is tight. Despite his eagerness, I don't think he wants to go down either.

"Wait. What happened down there? Tell us." I don't want to be caught unaware in the cellar, nor do I want to linger down there for story time.

Mason blinks rainwater out of his eyes, then runs a soaked sleeve across his face. "Nothing that I know of. The Lees almost forgot about it. They don't go down here."

"Why?" asks Nat. Mason shrugs.

"If we're going to do this, can we do it already?" Bethy asks. She's shaking, her teeth chattering, whether from fear or cold or a combination of the two, I can't tell.

Mason takes a deep breath and starts down the stairs. Nat and I go next, followed by Bethy, who sticks close to Conrad.

The stairs are ancient, made of unfinished wood that creaks and sags beneath our weight. The dirt floors at the base of the stairs are wet and muddy from rain. The cellar is only about six feet deep, which means Bethy and I are good for clearance, but both the guys and Nat have to watch out for support beams and exposed nails hanging down from the floor above. Down here, the storm seems distant, even with the cellar door open. But there's a gurgle of water that is out of place.

The house groans above us, as though we've entered the bowels of a living thing. To the right of the stairs, barely visible in the camera's light, is a hulking piece of rusted metal that looks vaguely like an ancient water heater. It must be out of commission, because there was a newer water heater behind the door in the utility room. The walls are hewn stone, fitted together with thick lines of mortar. The far wall, opposite the water heater, is lined with sagging wooden shelves bearing a couple dust-coated jars. Stone support pillars break our beam of light, casting the foreboding space beyond in darkness. Cobwebs ripple in the corners. The whole cellar is dirty and oppressive. No wonder the Lees don't come down here.

Tap, tap, tap. Conrad scans the darkened cellar with the camera, his light panning over it. The tapping is coming from somewhere beyond where the light reaches.

"Are the doors the only way to get down here?" Bethy asks in a whisper.

"Yeah. I mean, maybe there's a hole big enough for an animal to get in, but there aren't any other doors," Mason says. To the darkness, he calls out, "Hello? Is there anybody down here with us?"

The tapping stops, but there's no answer. Why would there be? It's not like ghosts have to reply and, if it's a person or animal, they wouldn't want us to find them. I inch closer to Nat.

"Rainwater?" I ask hopefully. I want to ask Nat what she feels, but she'll probably turn that question back on me, so I reluctantly close my eyes. My instincts scream to keep them open, making it difficult to focus.

With my eyes closed, I take a few deep breaths. My fear dissipates. Slowly. Slightly. I'm still scared, but the panic that had been tightening its hold on me lets go. It helps that Nat is a warm presence beside me, so I know I'm safe. Still, I'm convinced we're not entirely alone down here. It could just be a raccoon, or it could be a full-on apparition. Maybe a psycho killer. I'm not practised enough to know.

"What do you sense?" Nat whispers, low enough that Mason, who's crept over near the old water heater and is using a flashlight to search around it, doesn't hear.

I tap my thigh with my fingers, then open my eyes in defeat. "Nothing. I don't think we're alone down here, but I don't get more than that."

Her lips curve upwards in a slight smile that looks eerily inhuman in the shadows. Her eyes move over the darkness. "We're certainly not alone down here. This is an epicentre."

"Can you see them?"

"How do you know there's more than one?" Her gaze is distant.

"By the way you're acting. Your word choice."

She makes a *tsking* sound. "Here I thought you were rapidly improving your skills."

I bump her with my shoulder. "Just getting to know you better."

"Hey guys!" Mason yells, making me jump. "Check this out."

He's disappeared behind the old water heater. Bethy and Conrad have stuck close to Mason. Not close enough to disappear into the darkness after him, but close enough to keep him in the camera's frame. I guess he's more interesting for the channel than the two of us standing in the dark with our eyes closed.

"What?" Nat asks, hanging back. There isn't a lot of space between the stone wall and the rusted metal; maybe about a foot and a half.

"You need to see it. It's really cool." Mason's voice is high with excitement.

I inch past Nat and squeeze into the slight opening beyond the water heater. What had looked like a tight space is really quite open. Beyond two support beams is a small room with crumbling stone walls. Old hinges bolted to a rotting beam indicate that this area used to be closed off by a door or gate. Inside the room, a heavy stream of water runs from an open pipe down the wall and into the wide, black mouth of an open cistern. Maybe this was used as a water source for the house, once.

"Why isn't it covered?" I ask, keeping well away from the hole. "It seems dangerous."

Mason creeps closer, peering into the room, examining the walls with his flashlight.

"They keep the cellar padlocked. It's probably fine. It's not like there's a current or anything." He's standing on the narrow ledge of concrete along the side of the cistern, gripping the rough stone to keep from falling into the water half a foot below. He trains his light on the wall across the small room, up towards the ceiling. "What's that?"

"What?" we all ask in unison.

It looks like an old stone wall to me.

"That. Over there. Hold my phone." He hops off the ledge of the cistern onto the dirt floor, hands Bethy his phone, then walks to the other side, climbing onto the narrow ledge that's wet with rainwater. The concrete is slightly green with growth. The cistern must only water the garden. No one in their right minds would drink from it. "Can't you see it? The light reflects... right there."

He aims his flashlight so we can see the faint glimmer of something up in the corner of the wall, near the floorboards. It could be mica in the rock for all the shine it reflects. Mason stretches upwards, fingers scrabbling on rock. He takes a half step closer, his toes sliding on the slippery concrete. With a shriek, he falls backwards, and disappears beneath the dark surface with a splash. His flashlight stays lit for a second, then blinks out.

"Mason!"

Bethy is the first to the edge of the cistern. She leans over the water. White bubbles float to the surface, lit by the light of the camera. A couple seconds pass. Suddenly, Mason reappears below the surface. He comes up, spluttering and reaching for the edge. Bethy, Nat, and I grab him and haul him out of the cistern. He flops onto the dirt floor, landing on his hands and knees, coughing up water.

"Are you all right?" Nat pounds her palm against his back.

He wheezes between coughs. "Tell me you got that on camera?"

Conrad nods. "Of course I did. The camera was our only light source once you fell in."

"Good." Mason falls onto his back in the dirt, one arm above his head and the other across his heaving chest. "It'll make great clickbait."

"Is that all you care about?" I crouch beside him, arms crossed over my chest. "You could have died."

He winks at me, a grin creeping across his face. "I'm growing on you. Still glad you joined us?"

I roll my eyes, refusing to admit that I was scared when he went under.

"What do you think you saw?" Conrad asks, running the light of the camera along the walls. There *is* a faint glint in that one corner. "I don't think it's anything."

"No, there's something there. I'll get it this time." Again, Mason steps onto the narrow ledge. He inches forward, fingers gripping the stones.

"Mason, you're being an idiot." Bethy crosses her arms over her water-darkened sweater. "Don't think I'm pulling you out again."

This time, Mason doesn't try to avoid the steady stream of rainwater or the moisture on the stone, and holds himself close to the wall. He can't get any wetter. Fingers straining, he reaches up, clawing around the space until a sizeable chunk of stone shifts.

He ducks his head as it falls past him, glances off his shoulder, and lands in the water below.

Conrad trains the light on the hole in the wall. There's definitely something there. Mason reaches in, shouting. He keeps his head ducked, and pulls something loose from the wall, along with a lot of gravel and dust. He inches back along the ledge, finally jumping onto solid ground and dropping the age-worn, holey burlap sack at our feet.

"See? I told you there was something in the wall."

"Huh," Bethy says. "How did you see that?"

"I don't know. It just looked different. Maybe the house wanted me to find it."

CHAPTER EIGHT

Caroline Turner:
1860-1900

The children are up to their schemes again. The sound of fighting has made it up to even my rooms. I wish Gracie would keep her children in line. They are always picking on my sons. I know she suspects my relationship with my brother is untoward, though Philip Jr. and I have been careful to give her no reason to believe this. Still, her feelings are evident. Her children understand this and take it out on my dear Lester and Morris, without reason.

My hand glides along the banister as I descend the steps. My family home has aged well. I wish there was a way to guarantee it would pass to my sons and not Gracie's children. After all, my boys are full-blooded Turners. Gracie's are but half-Turner.

The door to the parlour is ajar. I look around, but Gracie and the nanny are nowhere to be found. I shake my head and take a deep breath, then glide into the room with all the fortitude I can summon. I admit, I am slightly terrified of Gracie's horde. Lester and Morris aren't the only ones they're disrespectful towards.

It is not the children I find when I enter the parlour; at least, not the children I expected to find. Morris is beside his brother, fiddling with his pocketknife, eyes trained on the floor. Lester stands in the centre of the room, a hatchet held above his head. His arms are trembling. Before him, Philip Jr. lies on the floor, half hidden by the settee. Gracie is bent over him. She hears me enter and looks up, her pretty face contorting in rage.

"Look what your sons have done!" she screams at me, blood spattered across her cheek.

Her eyes are wild. She looks nothing like the docile bride Philip Jr. brought home all those years ago. She holds out imploring hands to me, eyes darting to Lester, who still towers over her, hatchet raised. Blood covers her hands.

"They killed him!" she shrieks. "Do something!"

I take a step closer. I need to know, need to see with my own eyes. On the floor behind the settee, Philip Jr. is a crumpled shell of a man, his head of thick, sandy hair darkened with blood, half caved in. A dark pool has spread around him. Gracie's skirts are dark with it. My stomach drops, bile rising in my throat.

My breath comes out in a ragged sob. I lift trembling hands to cover my mouth. This can't be happening... Philip Jr., my soul-mate, my brother... is dead.

I turn to Lester, shaking. "What have you done?"

He doesn't look at me. His voice is rough. "I didn't mean to, but I can't take Aunt's comments anymore, Mama. She said…"

I take a step towards my eldest, my voice steely with rage. "What? What did she say?"

He licks his lips, and finally lowers the hatchet. "She said that I am an inbred bastard. Is it true?"

"So you killed your uncle?" I can't believe it. That horrible woman! Of course this was her fault. Everything is her fault.

"I wanted to help," Morris interrupts. "But Lester didn't need it."

"I didn't mean to, Mama!" Lester is crying now. "He jumped in front of Aunt Grace. I couldn't stop."

I close my eyes, my hands fisted at my sides. Never before have I wanted to hurt my child this badly. "You could have stopped," I hiss. "You've killed your own father! You are worthless!"

Lester looks at me with big, sad eyes. A lock of sandy Turner hair falls into his face, and in that second, everything shifts into place. I've been mistaken. My sons are not in the wrong. How could they be? They are mere children. Gracie had no right to speak to them like that. No right at all!

I rush around the settee, my shoes squelching in the pool of blood. Philip Jr.'s blood. I grab Gracie by the hair. It's long and glossy black, done up in an elaborate hairstyle that allows me a strong grip. Her hands reach for mine, eyes wide with shock. I hate her. I hate her! With all my might, I slam her towards the brick mantel.

The first blow lands with a dull thud. Her hands scrabble against mine. On the second blow, something crunches. Her hands fall limp, but I don't stop. I yank her back and slam her into the mantel again and again, until her beautiful face is caved in.

"Mama! Stop!" Lester's hands pull me back. I drop Gracie with an inelegant thud, breathing hard. "Please stop. Rosa's sent for the police."

All the blood drains from my face. I'd forgotten we weren't alone in the house. Gracie's children are a plague.

"I don't want to go to jail, Mama."

"And you won't. Stay quiet. You came in while I was doing this. I killed them both. You tried to stop me. Say nothing more than that. Do you understand?" My voice is raw. Lester stares at me in shock. He shakes like a leaf, but nods.

I'll take the fall for my sons, but I need to tell the truth, to this house of my forefathers, at the very least. My eyes land on the account book on the side table, a pen lying on the open page. That must have been the last thing Philip Jr. touched. I rush over to it and scribble a terse message, then take the bloodied hatchet and pocket knife from my sons. I will hide the evidence, fix this as best I can.

"Go wash your hands, Lester. You too, Morris. Know that Mama loves you and remember not to tell anyone anything else. I killed your aunt and uncle."

Lester nods, unmoving. Morris rocks back on his heels, staring at the two corpses on the floor.

"Go, boys!"

They turn and run from the room. I'm sure I only have minutes before the constable barges in. I must hurry. The evidence must be hidden somewhere it will never be found. Somewhere safe. The house will protect it, I'm sure.

My memories rush to the dirt cellar, where Philip Jr. and I used to spend long winter days playing, safe from Father's rage. I know just the place. Hurry! I must be quick.

·········

Present Day

A piece of stained, rusted metal sticks out through a hole in the burlap sack. I nudge the bundle with my toe. "Do you think it's smart to open this?"

Mason gives me a look that implies I'm an idiot and kneels in front of the bag. "Of course we're going to open it."

Conrad looks at me over the camera. "What Mason means to say is, 'You're right, Riley. It's a stupid idea to jump into something head first, but since I've already started, I'm going to keep going.' Right, Mason?"

"Yeah, yeah." Dirt cakes his clothes and his hair is straggly and stuck to his scalp, but he grins up at the camera, his teeth gleaming white. "This could be an amazing find, guys."

He's not talking to us, but to his future viewers. For his sake, I hope it's something reasonably cool and not a forgotten construction tool. As long as it's not a bag of bones, I'll be okay. I can't think of anything worse than finding body parts.

"Well, go on. Open it." Bethy crouches beside Mason, but far enough away that he can't get mud on her.

Nat leans towards me and asks in a low voice, "Does it feel different down here to you?"

I hadn't been paying attention, caught up instead in Mason's drama. I close my eyes and rock back on my heels, imitating Nat, trying to sense the atmosphere in the cellar. The air is quiet, the storm still muted, but there's an uneasiness that I can't place. It doesn't just have to do with the darkness beyond the camera's light. I open my eyes. "Yes, but I don't know how to describe it."

"It's like the house is holding its breath." She takes a step back from Mason. "*This* is one of its secrets."

"That's a good sign, then." Mason fumbles with the burlap, trying to find the opening. The seams are rotted and the rough fabric falls apart in his hands. He flips it back to reveal a rusted hatchet head stained black, a rotten piece of wood that could have been the hatchet's grip, a rusty knife with an ivory handle, and a leather-bound journal that has seen better days. Mason lets out a low whistle. "How old do you think this is?"

"When was the house built?" Conrad asks.

"1813. Do you think it's that old?" Mason picks up the hatchet head. "Should we ask the ghosts about this? What do you think the stains are?"

"Put it down," Nat says, in a low, dangerous voice.

"Why?" Mason asks.

"They're not yours." Nat is staring into the shadows beyond us.

I follow Nat's gaze and jump. A woman in a severe black dress is standing in the shadows, only partially visible. Her hair is light brown, almost blonde. She's not a full apparition. Parts of her fade in and out, but her face remains steady, her black eyes trained on us. On Mason and the artifacts, specifically. I swallow and take half a step back. If I can see her, does this mean my guard is dropping? Or is she that powerful?

"What?" Conrad turns to look behind him, the camera panning over the darkness. "What do you see?"

"A woman," I say. Nat glances at me, but I keep my eyes fixed on the apparition. If Nat sees it too, then it can't be my imagination. This is not good. "You can't see her?"

"No." He zooms the camera in.

"What does she look like?" Mason asks, craning his head to peer into the shadows.

I take a slow breath, not daring to move. "Dark dress, light hair, white. Angry."

She flickers, then reappears next to Mason.

"They must stay safe." Her ghost voice is a whisper, almost drowned out by the trickle of water and distant rush of wind. *"It is a secret. Put it back."*

"She wants you to put it back," Nat tells Mason.

"You both see it?" Mason jumps to his feet, squinting into the darkness. "I don't see anything."

"Me either," Bethy says. "But if she wants us to put this back, I think we should."

"No." Nat steps towards the ghost, stepping between it and the scrap of fabric on the floor. The ghost's eyes flick to her, unnaturally fast. "No, we won't put it back. This needs to come out for you to rest. This cannot hurt you. You are beyond hurt now. It'll be good for you."

"Are they dead?" The ghost frowns, her expression darkening. *"No."*

She flickers a few times, then blinks out of sight.

"Who is she?" I ask Nat.

Nat shrugs and stoops to examine the contents of the sack. "I don't know, but I think we'll find out."

"If we're not putting it back, can we at least take it upstairs where we can look at it with the lights on?" Bethy asks. "This place is freaking me out."

· · · · ● · ● · · · ·

"Do not start without me!" Mason's thumping around in the bathroom, as though there's a battle going on between him and his jeans. There might very well be. His jeans were soaked through and tighter than the average pair. He's made us promise to wait for him until he changes into fresh clothes.

Bethy spins around on a barstool at the kitchen island. "Seriously, Mason! You're taking forever."

The rest of us are gathered around the kitchen, our clothes still damp from the rain. I have clothes in the car, but I don't want to let anyone know that. Aside from Conrad, who already knows I'm living in my car. Besides, we're not wet enough to need a change. The rain was heavy, but it only soaked my shoulders. None of us fell in a cistern.

The sack is caked in dirt. We didn't want to mess up the Lee's house any more than we already have, so we laid it out across some newspapers we found in the recycling bin. The top page mentions the missing woman, still no leads.

"You didn't peek, did you?" Mason asks, entering the kitchen. He's changed into another pair of jeans and a black T-shirt. His hair is mussed from a towel, but clearly styled so he's presentable for the camera.

Nat gestures to the sack. "We'll let you do the honours. You risked your neck for it."

"Awesome." Mason rubs his hands together. "Ready, Connie?"

"Don't call me that." Conrad picks up the camera and steps back so we're all in the shot. "I'm good."

Mason unfolds the burlap and reaches inside, bits of dirt and gravel falling onto the newspaper. He pulls out the four items we saw while we were in the cellar, then feels around for anything else. He withdraws his hand with a frown. "I guess this is it."

In the bright lights of the kitchen, the hatchet looks even worse for wear. In addition to the rust dulling the blade, there are darker stains on the metal. Some of this stuff flakes off when Mason picks it up.

"I think that's blood," Bethy says.

"Really?" Mason's face lights up. "That's amazing. Do you think it's human or animal?"

Nat grimaces but doesn't answer.

"Judging from the way the ghost was acting, I'm going to guess human," I say.

Nat nods approvingly at me. "I agree."

Mason pulls his hand back, then reaches out to turn the hatchet over. "I wonder whose it is. What did the woman look like? Why could you see her and not us?"

"Riley's sensitive, remember? I think tonight is giving her a crash course on her abilities." Bracing her elbow on the countertop, Nat uses her hand to shield her eyes from the overhead light, as though it's causing her pain.

"That is so cool. I wish I could do that." Mason gazes at me, still fiddling with the hatchet head.

"Mason," Conrad says. "Maybe you should put that down. If it's blood, we should probably have someone look at it."

"What can they do? It's ancient." Still, he sets the piece of metal back on the newspaper and picks up the piece of wood. It's tapered on one end, as though it once fit through the hatchet head, before time and Mason's rough handling caused it to fall out. There are dark stains on the wood, though the middle is clear of staining, just darkened with age and rot. "Do you think the clean part is where the killer—I'm assuming that's where we're going with this—held the hatchet?"

He places his hand in the clean area. The clean space covers more of the handle than his hand does. He frowns.

"The killer had pretty big hands if we're assuming that," Bethy says. She stands up to get her water bottle. "Are we going to ask the ghost?"

"Wait." Conrad sets the camera down. "Bethy, you have tiny hands. Come here."

"Yeah, and that is a big clean spot. Do I have to?" Despite her protests, she reluctantly comes to Conrad's side.

He takes the handle and places both her hands on the wooden shaft, one above the other. It makes more sense than Mason's single-handed grip. "If the killer was smaller and needed more strength, they would have had to use both hands. What if we're looking at a woman or child?"

"But no one was killed with a hatchet here." Mason pulls out his phone and scrolls through his notes. "There's no history to match."

"There's no *recorded* history." I don't want to be a part of this. Something is telling me we're getting into something dangerous, bigger than ourselves. "You've got the hatchet and the knife. That means that something happened with both. Maybe they're hunting tools."

"Then why hide them? Maybe it's an early serial killer or something." Bethy drops the handle on the table and rubs her hands on her pants as she takes her seat. "I hope that's not human blood."

"It might not be blood at all." Conrad picks up the camera again. "That's why we need to get these things analyzed."

Mason picks up the knife and turns it over in his hand. Time has dulled and rusted the blade to where it would be useless for anything other than buttering bread, but at one time, it was probably someone's prized possession.

"What does the journal say?" Nat asks, uncovering her eyes for the first time in several minutes. Her face is haggard and drawn, with dark circles under her eyes.

"Are you okay?" I ask. "You don't look so good."

Her grim smile doesn't reach her eyes. "Just getting old, I suspect. These all-nighters aren't as easy as they used to be."

I don't believe her. There's an uneasiness here. We'd talked about it before. Is the house taking its toll on her? It's affecting me, too. I haven't felt fully at peace for hours now.

Mason flips through the journal. The pages are brittle and bits fall off them.

"You're wrecking it. Give it to me." Bethy holds out her hand. After a few moments of hesitation, Mason gives it to her. She sets it down on the table and opens it slowly, turning the pages gently, one at a time. "It looks like an account book. It's hard to read, super faded."

I walk around the table to peer over her shoulder. She's right. The pencil has faded, making the numbers almost illegible. The handwriting is cramped, the vowels between consonants more squiggle than letters. Halfway through the book, she stops. Bold, black letters, written in ink and surrounded by splotches, are scrawled across the page.

I killed her, but I would never kill my brother. I do this to save our sons. Forgive me.

"What does that mean? I do this to save our sons—do what?" Bethy reads aloud. "Who wrote that?"

"And who hid murder weapons in the cistern?" Conrad asks.

With a clatter, Mason drops the knife he's been playing with. "Murder weapons? You guys seriously think these were used to kill someone?"

"What about two someones?" Nat asks. She's resting her head on her hand, her eyes closed. She's pale and looks exhausted. Something isn't right and I'm betting it's the house. My stomach churns. "Whoever wrote this admits to one murder, but who killed the brother? Is this that brother and sister with the inbred sons? Are those the sons the writer is protecting? Lester and...?"

"Morris," Mason says. "Caroline's sons."

"I'm willing to bet Caroline is the writer. Do you think the sons had something to do with killing *her*? Is that what the author was protecting them from?"

"But Philip Jr. was killed with a fire poker, not a hatchet or knife." Mason scrolls through his phone and pulls up the information. "See. It says right here."

There's a picture in his notes of a woman. She's the same woman I saw in the cellar. My stomach flips and my hands tremble. "Who's that woman?"

"Caroline. Her picture was in the newspaper after her arrest."

I look at Nat, needing confirmation. She nods, lifting her head out of her hand. "You're right."

"Right about what?" Bethy asks.

I point at the picture on Mason's phone. "That is the woman I saw."

Chapter Nine

"We don't use the voice recorder as often as we should," Bethy says, closing the door to Eric's room behind us. I set the camera in an empty spot on the bookshelf, where it will catch most of the room.

I sit on the edge of the bed, careful not to muss the covers. She sits beside me, placing the flashlight, our only light source aside from the gleam of the camera, between us. After determining that the woman Nat and I saw in the cellar was Caroline, we've decided to do a session with just Bethy and me. If the history is true, and Caroline was self-confined to the house, maybe less people will encourage her to talk with us. The others are sitting out on the verandah, leaving the house to us.

"Mason doesn't like doing EVPs. I think it bores him, having to pause between questions, then listen back. I think EVPs are more compelling than the spirit box, even."

I touch the small, gray rectangle of the voice recorder. "I've seen you use this in your videos. You ask a question and wait a few seconds before asking another?"

"Yep. Then you listen back to see if you can hear any noise you know wasn't in the room." She settles back onto the bed. "Get comfortable. You don't want to move while it's recording or we might think the rustle of fabric is a voice."

I shuffle further back onto the bed. "I'm ready."

She clicks the record button. "Hello. Is there anyone in here with us?"

She pauses before continuing. "What is your name?"

Another pause.

"What happened in this house?"

After a few seconds, she turns to me. "Should we listen?"

I nod, leaning forward to hear the playback.

The quality of the recording isn't great, but Bethy's voice is strong.

"Is there anyone in here with us?"

"Yes." The word sounds distorted, as though someone is talking too close to the microphone.

She looks at me. "That was a clear yes."

I nod, motioning for her to continue. She presses play.

"What is your name?"

Static answers. She rewinds. We put our heads together to hear it better. Again, static fills the air, but I can tell it's a word. The voice rises and falls.

"Three syllables? Maybe Caroline?" I ask.

Bethy shrugs. "No way to be sure."

She presses play for the final question.

"What happened in this house?"

"Death."

I shiver. There was no mistaking that word.

"Let's ask more questions," Bethy says. "You ask this time."

"All right."

She presses record, then nods at me.

Nervous, I rack my brain for questions, settling on the most obvious. "You said death happened here. Who died?"

I count to ten. "We didn't catch your name. Can you say it clearer?"

Another ten count. "Are you happy here?"

I look at Bethy. She raises her eyebrows in question. At my nod, she stops the recorder, and replays our answers.

"-death happened here. Who died?"

"Ev-ry one."

The word is stilted, but clear enough. My palms are cold and damp.

"We didn't catch your name. Can you say it clearer?"

"C—ine."

Bethy pauses the recording, plays it back, but it sounds no clearer. "It's saying a name. Something that starts with a 'ka' sound and ends with an 'n', but I can't make it out. It could be Caroline."

"Maybe, but it could be that first wife, too. The one Mason mentioned. I think he said her name was Katherine?"

Bethy nods as she considers this. "It could be. It would fit. We're talking to one of those women for sure. Let's continue."

She presses play.

"Are you happy?"

"No."

Bethy looks at me. "We have to see if we can help."

I nod, motioning towards the voice recorder. "Ask."

She presses record, and I hold my breath, listening for whispers.

"Why aren't you happy?"

Silent seconds pass.

"Do you need help?"

More silence. The darkness in the room presses in against us. The flashlight seems to grow dimmer. I look at Bethy. She shrugs.

"How can we help you?"

The air shifts in the room, growing chilly. If this happens while Eric is sleeping, it's no wonder he ends up on his sister's floor most nights.

"Did you feel that?" Bethy asks.

I nod. "Something happened."

"Let's listen back."

She presses play.

"Why aren't you happy?"

"Couldn't be."

I frown, still not sure who we're talking to, though I'm inclined to think it's Katherine. In the cellar, Caroline had seemed more angry than sad. Whoever we're talking to here sounds depressed.

"Do you need help?"

There's no answer, just dead air. This is when the energy shifted, became darker. Goosebumps prickle my arms. Had something stopped this spirit from answering us?

"How can we help you?"

"RAAAHH!"

A low, furious bellow roars through the voice recorder. I jump, nearly falling off the edge of the bed. Bethy fumbles to catch the recorder.

"What was that?" I ask. I do not need jump scares tonight.

She turns off the recorder. The quiet should be peaceful, but this room doesn't feel safe. "Someone's angry. Let's go find the others."

Bethy crosses the room to pick up the camera. I turn to smooth out the covers. The chill doesn't let up, but I do my best to ignore the sensation that there's someone standing behind me.

THUMP.

"What was that?" Bethy asks, panning the room with her flashlight.

"I thought it was you." I straighten, scanning the room for anything that might have fallen.

"No, I was standing still, waiting for you."

My eyes land on the floor near the desk. The football. It's rocking gently on the carpet. I point at it. "The football. It was on the desk."

Neither Bethy nor I are near the desk.

"Maybe our movements knocked it off? The floor shifted or something?"

"There's no way it fell now and not when the five of us were in here earlier. It has to be..." I inch towards the door. "Should we leave?"

"Yeah. That's a good idea. Let's meet the others on the verandah." She follows me out of the room, calling over her shoulder, "Bye for now."

·· · · • • · • • · ·

"You're back!" Mason leaps from the porch swing. Conrad and Nat struggle to stop the swing from crashing against the wall of the house. "What happened?"

The air is cold and damp, refreshing and alive, after our experience upstairs.

"You're both pale," Conrad says, finally slowing the swing. "Want to sit?"

He and Nat make room for us, while Mason hovers about, barely able to contain his excitement. Beyond the overhanging roof of the verandah, the rain pelts the earth with fury. The wind whips around the corners of the house, making even this sheltered area chilly. Still, it's preferable to the house. The air, though thick with moisture, is lighter out here.

"So?" Mason asks.

"We got responses from someone," Bethy says. "I'm not sure if it was Caroline."

"Just listen and tell us what you think."

Bethy presses play on the recording. They all lean in to hear over the rain. When we get to the part where we ask a second time for a name, Nat holds up a finger. Bethy pauses it.

"Play it again?"

Bethy rewinds a few seconds, then plays it again. She pauses it. Conrad frowns, leaning closer to the recorder.

"It's hard to tell. It could be Caroline, but I think it's closer to Katherine. The middle syllable is practically inaudible, though."

"That's what I thought too," I say. "Katherine was the name of the first Turner woman who lived here, right?"

Mason frowns, but pulls his phone out and scrolls through his notes. "Right. She was Joseph's wife."

"Keep listening. We haven't got to the best part yet." Bethy plays the recording again.

Mason leans in, intent. He nods each time the ghost says something, frowns at the second-to-last question, which went unanswered, then leans in even closer for the last.

"How can we help you?"

"RAAAHH!"

"Ah!" He jumps back, grabbing his chest. "That's terrifying. Who screamed at you?"

Bethy turns off the recorder. "Who knows? I think the screamer sounded male."

Nat nods. "And angry. Was that the end? Did anything else happen?"

"The room seemed heavier when we asked 'Do you need help?' and then when we asked 'How can we help you?' it got really cold," I say. "We heard nothing until we listened back."

"But..." Bethy says, dramatic flair in her voice. She pauses until Mason is squirming with anticipation.

"But what?" he whines.

"As we were getting ready to leave the room..." Another pause to torment Mason.

"What happened?"

"The football on Eric's desk fell to the floor."

"That's it?" Mason lets out an exasperated sigh. "You probably bumped it."

"No. We were nowhere near it."

"And," I cut in, "there were five of us up there earlier, and it didn't fall then. I'm positive the ghost knocked it off the desk."

"Let me see the video." Mason grabs the camera from beside Bethy. He sinks into a sitting position on the floor and fiddles with the camera's controls, then scrutinizes the tiny screen. I can hear the thump of the football and Bethy asking what that was. Mason looks up at us, his brow furrowed. "You didn't catch the football falling on camera. The camera was pointed at the wall!"

Bethy shrugs. "We were about to leave. I had my hands full."

"Bethy!" Mason wails. "You always miss the good parts!"

"All right, Mason." Conrad stands. "Let's keep going. You've got a lot of good evidence on camera tonight. You can't blame Bethy for not knowing what the ghost was going to do before he did it."

He nudges Mason's leg with the toe of his shoe. "Up and at 'em."

·········

The kitchen is dark except for the light from the camera. Conrad leans against the counter, pointing his camera at the island where we're all seated, the murder weapons and account book in the centre.

Mason turns on the spirit box and places it next to the items. He's checked them all over with the EMF detector and nothing happened, so we know the items themselves aren't haunted. The spirit box fills the room with a steady pulse of static that I'm starting to hate. I rub my temples. There's a sharp pain blooming there.

"Caroline Turner, if you're here, we would like to talk to you. We have some questions about the acts that led to your death." Mason's face is thrown into contrast by light and shadows, the green of his eyes shining. His once damp hair has dried into a frizzy mass about his head, creating a halo-like affect. "You can speak to us through this device."

"This noisy, annoying device," Conrad mutters.

Mason gestures around the kitchen, where the flashlights, EMF detector and cat ball are set up. "If you're here, can you give us some sort of sign?"

The wind sighs around the house, but inside it's still—until the pots above the island rattle together. Conrad jumps away from them with a low swear, training the camera on the movement. "I guess she's here."

"Caroline, can you confirm that your sons, Lester and Morris, were the ones responsible for the deaths of Philip Jr. and his wife Gracie?"

I stare across the table at Bethy, who's playing with the ends of her hair, twisting it between her fingers. She chews on her lower lip.

"They deserved it." The words are crystal clear, coming through the spirit box over the static.

Bethy looks up, and her wide eyes meet mine. "They deserved it—who are we speaking to? Can you give us a name?"

"Let her."

"Let her what?" Mason asks.

"No." Nat reaches across the island towards Mason, tapping the granite. "Lester."

His eyes widen and his jaw drops. "Are we talking to Lester Turner? Can you turn on the flashlight beside Conrad if this is you?"

With no hesitation, the flashlight beside Conrad blinks on. Conrad lets out a shaky breath.

"Did you kill Philip Jr. and Gracie?" Mason asks. "You said they deserved it."

"Mean... hurt her..."

"Mean? Hurt her? Did you kill them because they hurt your mother, Caroline?"

"Yesss..."

Mason runs a hand through his hair, making it stand up even more. "Did your mother take the fall for you? They hung her because of what you did."

"Morris…" The sentence doesn't finish, but the implication is clear. Morris killed them.

I gasp as a thought comes to me. "Morris died in a fire. Did you start the fire to get rid of him?"

"That's random," Bethy says. "What made you think of that?"

I shrug, about to answer that I don't know, when the spirit box answers.

"Guilty."

Mason leans across the table, whispering as though the ghost won't be able to hear. "Does that mean both brothers were murderers? Is Lester guilty, or Morris?" Then, louder, he asks, "Lester, did you kill your brother?"

The energy in the room shifts.

"I'm not feeling good," Nat says. She leans forward and rests her head on her arms.

"What's wrong?" Bethy asks.

I place a hand on her shoulder. She's hot to the touch. "Should we stop?"

A low voice moans from the spirit box. *"Gooo."*

Above the kitchen island, the pots rattle again. Conrad jerks the camera up to catch their movement. But in the darkness, they're still. He strides over to the wall and flicks on the light, catching a slight sway that could have been caused by his footsteps. Suddenly, a door slams upstairs. Mason looks at us for a second, the whites of his eyes showing, then bolts out of the kitchen, the soles of his shoes slapping against the hardwood. Conrad rushes behind him, camera in hand.

"We're done talking to you for now," Bethy says quickly and turns off the spirit box. The silence that follows is a balm, even with the rush of the storm outside. The tension in my body lifts a little.

"Do you need anything?" I ask Nat.

She rubs her brow, massages her temples. "I feel better with that thing off. It's this house. There's something dark here. It doesn't like us learning its secrets, but they need to come out. The family won't have peace until they do."

A breeze blows through the room, despite the windows and doors being closed. Bethy looks over her shoulder, then rounds the island to sit beside Nat and me.

"Should we leave?" she asks in a whisper.

Nat nods. "I would like to, but I don't know if we can convince Mason."

We're interrupted by Mason's high-pitched shriek, followed by two sets of footsteps pounding overhead, then thundering down the stairs. I jump out of my stool, the legs scraping against the floor, and rush towards the entryway and the base of the stairs. Bethy gets there before me. Mason pushes past her, almost knocking her over.

Conrad stops on the bottom step. His chest is heaving, his face paler than I've seen it. "Mason."

Mason stops with his hand on the knob of the front door. He turns to us, his face pale and drawn. "Grab your stuff. We're out of here."

I frown, wanting to ask what could have scared him so badly, but I keep my mouth shut. This might be my only chance to bow out early. And Nat said we should leave. I pull my keys out of my jeans pocket. My phone is in my back pocket. I'm good to go.

"Wait," Bethy says. "What scared you? You screamed like a little girl."

Mason's mouth drops. He snaps it shut. "I did not. I'll tell you when we're out of here."

He yanks open the door to the verandah. The yard is a swamp, the rain so heavy I can barely make out the shape of my car in the driveway. The wind whips the rain sideways, creating a mist that immediately makes me damp, even though I'm standing well out of reach of the downpour.

"I don't think it's safe to drive in this," Conrad yells over the wind.

"What?" Mason yells back.

The hairs on the back of my neck rise. I look around. Is this a ghost thing?

A blazing bolt of light cracks across the sky. The air sizzles. Ozone burns my nostrils. Thunder explodes around us. I drop to my knees, hands over my ears, eyes clamped shut.

Mason and Conrad are shouting, barely audible over the ringing in my ears. I open my eyes, but am night-blind from the lightning. As I blink away the spots, a hand grabs my forearm. Bethy is pulling me to my feet, saying something I can't hear. She points out the door, across the lawn. I follow the line of her finger, then step numbly out onto the verandah.

My car is gone. The top half of a giant oak lies where it once was. Conrad's SUV is partially covered by the branches as well. Nat puts a hand on my shoulder and turns me back to the house, Bethy close behind.

I slump onto the entry bench, not caring about the ghosts right now. My car was my home. It was all I had. More than that, it was the car that Riley and I drove into the wee hours of the night. The car we took beach trips in. It was more than just a car to me. It was memories.

"What are we going to do?" Bethy asks in a small voice. She's standing in front of me, arms crossed over her chest, glancing up the stairs nervously.

Nat rubs circles on my back. The motion slowly pulls me back to myself. It reminds me of my mom, from when I was small, before everything changed. It's reassuring.

Maybe the car won't be completely destroyed. Maybe it'll be fine underneath the tree. I take a deep breath and sit upright. Either way, there's nothing I can do about it right now. Nat pats my back, then stretches her arms out in front of her, letting out a sigh.

"The guys can debate it all they want. Even if they can get the SUV out from under the tree, they can't drive it around the branch. The front yard is fenced in. Even if it wasn't, the grass is too wet to drive on."

"So, we're stuck here?" Bethy moves to the narrow window beside the front door and peers out. "I thought you said we should leave."

"I think we should leave, but it's obviously not safe to walk in this weather and the cars are inaccessible. I'm not going to sit in the SUV and wait for another tree to come down. It looks like the choice to stay has been made for us." She stretches out her legs and leans back against the wall.

"Aren't you scared?" I ask.

She shrugs. "It's better not to be scared in these situations. The spirits feed off our energy. Fear is a powerful emotion. I'm not giving it away."

The door opens and Conrad walks in. Mason slinks in after him, glancing nervously down the hall.

"You okay, Mase?" Nat asks, turning her head to look at him without lifting it off the wall.

He's still a little wild, his eyes wide and face pale. The wind has done no favours for his hair, either.

"What were you so scared of?" Bethy asks, touching his arm.

He jumps, glances up the stairs, then at Conrad. "We saw a full-on apparition."

Conrad nods. "He's not lying. Full on person. No shadows or wispiness. I got it on camera."

He fiddles with the camera, then holds it out, turning so we can all see the screen. It's hard to see anything on a small screen when the footage is dark, but the form of a person walking down the hallway and disappearing at the end is unmistakable. "I thought it was one of you at first, playing a trick on us. Then I realized the size didn't fit. This is a man."

"Is that a ghost?" Bethy leans in towards the screen.

Nat peers at the screen. "Not one that I've met tonight."

"Who do you think it was? Lester?" I ask. The house hadn't been comfortable before, but it's even less so now. A tapping sound from the kitchen has me glancing over my shoulder before I realize it's rain on the windows.

Conrad shrugs. He's not the kind of guy given to suppositions. "We only saw his back. We didn't interact with him at all."

"What made the noise? Did you figure that out?" Bethy shifts from foot to foot, glancing up at the shadowy darkness at the top of the stairs.

"There was a closed door, but it could have been a draft. It's an old house and with that storm outside—"

"It wasn't a draft," Mason says. Like Bethy, he can't stand still. He fists both hands in his hair, scrunches his face in consternation. "I want to leave."

"We're not going anywhere, Mase." Conrad puts an arm around Mason's shoulders and gives him a brief hug. "We discussed it outside. Until the storm passes, and we can get the tree off the cars, we're stuck here."

"But..."

"All right." Nat slaps her thighs and stands. "Enough of this. We've got the house to ourselves and have promised the Lees we would investigate. We have enough evidence to prove that it's haunted, but all we've done so far is stir things up. Part of that might be the storm. Let's see if we can't make reparations with the spirits so the Lees aren't walking back into a war zone."

I can't tell if she has a plan or if this is simply a way to mitigate our fears, stop us from feeding the spirits. After all, dawn is still hours away. That's a long time to huddle in fear. I'd rather do something than shiver in misery all night.

"How do you settle a haunted house?" I ask.

Chapter Ten

Nat leads us into the living room and turns on the lamps in front of the windows.

"Take a seat," she tells us. I slump onto the couch beside Bethy and Conrad. Nat sits on the chair beside me, leaving Mason the chair across from her, furthest from us. Nat places her palms on her knees and takes a deep breath, tilting her head to either side, her neck popping. Is the house still affecting her?

I rub my palms on my jeans. "How do we fix this house?"

"We can't," Mason says. "Even Nat can't do it on her own. Right, Nat?"

Nat shrugs, her eyes moving around the room, as though seeing things I can't. I let my eyes unfocus and I take in the room as a whole, rather than bits of separate items, like furniture, decor, and us. Shadows shift beyond us, but it's hard to tell if it's my imagination or if there is actually a spirit or something there. My stomach twists uncomfortably. At this point it might be hunger.

It's been several hours since I last ate, but the constant unease and frequent fear is keeping me from feeling hunger cues.

"What do you see?" Bethy asks Nat. Her voice trembles and I remember what Nat said about fear. I straighten my shoulders, not letting myself give in to that basic survival mechanism. There is nothing for me to fear here, not surrounded by my friends with Nat on the lookout for us. The thought surprises me, but it's true. These people are my friends.

Nat smiles at Bethy, but ignores her question. She answers mine instead. "Without the resident's permission, it's hard to fix a haunted home, but it helps that we've been invited in. We can let the spirits know that we're here with permission. They might not know they're dead. If that's the case, we seem like the intruders to them. We can explain who we are, what we're doing here and let them know the current situation. Sometimes that's enough for them to pass on. Sometimes it settles them enough that the residents of the house will only hear the occasional footsteps or creaking of a door. In this case, with vases smashing and so many things moving around—"

"Apparitions," Mason interrupts.

Nat nods. "Yes, apparitions—it might take more for us to appease the spirits. The Lees might need to declare the house theirs and smudge it. Maybe a priest should be called in, but the house isn't ours, so we can't do that tonight."

"So, what do we need to do?" I ask.

"Just what we've done before. But this time, we don't want to stir them up. Close your eyes, take a few deep breaths. Calm yourself."

I follow her instructions, letting myself relax back into the couch. It's hard to keep my eyes closed. My back is to the door. The darkness of the house is behind me, looming, empty. Anything could come through. I focus my attention on my breathing, matching my inhales with the breaths of the others. My limbs are heavy and exhausted, the late night catching up with me.

"Are there any spirits here with us?" Nat asks once we've all followed her instructions and are sitting with our eyes closed in the dimly lit room. Her voice is clear and strong.

A cool breeze caresses my face. I suck in a quick breath, but don't flinch. It's just a draft, not a spirit.

"Riley?" Nat asks. Without opening my eyes, I know that her attention is on me.

"I'm fine," I say, realizing that I mean it. I'm not afraid right now. Sure, I'm unsettled, but I'm gradually relaxing. "Just a draft."

"Mhmm." Nat doesn't say more than that, but I can tell she knows it's more than an air current. To the room, she says, "I know you're here. Thank you for listening to me."

She pauses. Then says, "I know you're agitated. We've come into your home with our devices and have stirred up your energies. I want to make sure you know that you are no longer on the physical plane. Your spirits can move on if you will let them. There is a family here that has asked us to come investigate this house. It's a wonderful house. We're thankful they let us come. I know you all spent time here in the past. It was your home, but it's now time to let the living live. The current family is frightened of you. They have two children they want to protect. I won't say that you can stay here. They may want you gone. If you want a chance to stay, you need to make yourselves known as pleasant and peaceful, so they know their children are safe."

A breeze blows through the room, against the back of my neck. I can't help but open my eyes. Bethy shifts on the couch beside me, then opens her eyes too. I glance over my shoulder, but the front door isn't open, nor are any of the windows. My eyes meet Bethy's. Her pupils are blown wide, black in the light of the lamps.

The lights in the room flicker. The shadows loom as the bulbs almost go out, but the lights come back on. I let out a sigh of relief, just as a bolt of lightning flashes across the sky, lighting up the windows behind the sheer curtains. The crash of thunder that follows is almost deafening. The power lines hum as the lights grow brighter, then sizzle into darkness.

Mason leaps from his chair. "Was that them?"

Nat shakes her head. "The storm."

I can't see anything. My eyes had grown used to the light, and now we're in pitch darkness. Even the streetlamps across the lawn have gone dark. I hear someone—Mason, I think—shuffle across the room and try the light switch.

"Power's out, Mase," Conrad says. "Use your flashlight."

Mason's flashlight clicks on, blinding me. I blink, raising a hand to shield my eyes, and glance about the room. It should be frightening, being stuck here in the dark with a house full of ghosts and spirits. But I'm not scared. Whatever peace Nat has inspired in me lingers. I don't know why I was so scared before, but I'm grateful for the reprieve.

Mason looks terrified.

"Aren't you used to the dark?" I ask. "All the hunts I watched have been in the dark."

For a moment, he seems to forget where we are. He lights up. "You watched our videos?"

I shrug and look down at my hands, glad it's dark enough to hide my hot ears. "Some of them. I wanted to make sure I wasn't getting in with a crowd of serial killers."

Conrad reaches over Bethy to ruffle my hair. A warm ball of happiness grows in my chest. I wonder if this is what having an older brother would've been like. It's been a long time since I felt like I belonged anywhere, a long time since there was somewhere I could call home. These people have their flaws, but it's nice to be a part of their group. I want this sense of belonging to last.

"I wish the lights would come on," Mason grumbles. "It's one thing choosing to film in darkness. I don't like not having the option of lights. And we can't even leave."

"Mason," Nat says in a soothing tone, as though this has happened before. "It's a power outage. There's a storm. The lights will come on once the power company can fix it."

"Judging by the storm, that could take a while," Bethy mutters, but I don't think Mason hears. He's pacing in front of the fireplace with his flashlight.

"Sit down, Mason." Conrad stretches out his legs and crosses his arms.

Mason drops into his chair, but continues to scan the room with his flashlight.

Nat shakes her head, then closes her eyes and says, "I would like to help you cross over, if that is something you are interested in. I will open a space on the wall above the mantel, a thinning of sorts, or a portal. On the other side is the spiritual plane. If you would like to cross over peacefully and of your own accord, I urge you to go now."

I watch her twist her hands as though pulling the delicate cords of a blind, and imagine the wall coming down.

There's a flicker of ethereal green light, then another, as though the spirits are passing over, flaring on the threshold. I shake my head. Maybe it's the exhaustion, or maybe I'm going crazy. I can't really be seeing this. It has to be my imagination.

"Last chance, all," Nat says, holding her hands in the air like an orchestra conductor drawing out a note. "I'm closing the portal in three... two... one."

She reverses the graceful dance of her hands. As she does so, the room loses something. It seems drier, fresher. Less haunted. I take in a deep breath, surprised to find that my heart is racing, and my hands are clammy. It isn't fear, but some visceral response to whatever just happened.

I look at the others. Bethy is whispering to Conrad, who is grinning and nodding at what she's saying. Mason picks at his nails, his brow furrowed as he glances about the room. They don't seem to notice any change.

Nat dusts off her hands as though this task has left residue, and looks at us. She takes in the behaviour of the others, then stops on me. She raises an eyebrow.

"What was that?" I ask.

She shrugs. "Just what I said it was. You can feel the difference?"

I nod, not knowing what to say. I know all of the ghosts can't possibly have gone in such a short time. How would they have heard Nat if they were in the attic or cellar? What about the girl upstairs? I don't want her to be stuck here forever. "Are they all gone? Even the girl in the attic?"

"There are still spirits here, but not with us right this minute. The ones who wanted to leave left. I'm sure she went with them." Her brow furrows. "The darkness is still here. I wish I could figure out what it is. It doesn't feel human, but that doesn't mean much. Spirits can portray themselves as something they're not, much like we can pretend to be someone we're not."

I ignore that pointed comment and suppress a shiver. Fear is a funny creature. I shouldn't be afraid of something that can't hurt me. How much damage can a ghost really do? They can scratch people, I know that from my time spent online, but they can't outright kill a person, can they? I suppose they could throw someone down the stairs, like they tried to do with me. So, I have reason to be afraid, but if what Nat says is true, I have some sort of power over them at the same time. I wish I had my old cross necklace, but as far as I know, it's in my pink jewelry box at home.

"So what do we do now?" Mason asks. "It seems stupid to sit around and do nothing when the Lees loaned us their house for the night."

"It'll be morning before you know it. I'm sure they'll be happiest if we don't stir up more activity for them," Nat replies.

"But we could still look around and see if we can catch anything for the channel, can't we?"

"Weren't you the one running scared and yelling for the rest of us to follow just a few minutes ago?" Bethy asks. She's snuggled into Conrad's side, with his arm draped over her shoulder, and doesn't look inclined to move. She looks up at her boyfriend. "Please tell me you got his moment of desperation on camera? The fans will love that. Can you imagine the memes?"

"Ha ha. Hilarious." Mason slumps back in his chair, but still looks at Conrad for his answer.

"I got every moment—from freaking out after seeing the apparition, to nearly falling down the stairs in his rush to get out, to running out into the storm and almost leaving us all behind." Conrad's casual drawl is tinged with humour.

"Good. I look forward to editing this video." Bethy sinks back against Conrad.

"You do the editing?" I'm surprised. She looks too preppy and pretty to have computer skills.

She smirks. "It's not like it's all that hard. They're just simple videos. Are you implying I don't look geeky enough? I have purple hair."

"That's pretty cool." My first impression of Bethy was wrong. I already liked her, but my estimation of her just went up. She's got some skills to go along with her attitude. And she's nice. Riley would approve.

"Seriously," Mason says. "Are we just going to sit around all night? This is boring."

"What do you want to do, Mase?" Conrad asks in a laid-back voice. "Nat doesn't want us stirring things up."

"We could just sit quietly, couldn't we? Do our usual solo time."

I'd seen the solo times in some of their videos. They look pretty creepy, sitting around in the dark, alone except for the spirits. Usually Mason tries to provoke them, while Conrad just chills and investigates whatever area he's stuck in. Bethy interacts with the spirits and spooks herself. I hadn't seen Nat in any videos, so I don't know what her process is, but I'd like to find out.

Everyone looks to Nat for her opinion. She narrows her eyes at Mason. "I think we've done enough. There are kids that live here. We can wait out the storm in here."

"Sure. Or we could sit quietly in another part of the house. What's going to happen?"

Nat shrugs. "Who knows? Do you really want to test it?"

"Yeah. I do." Mason springs to his feet. "Let's go."

Nat sighs. "Fine."

"Who's going first?" Bethy asks.

"We've got enough cameras, and the house is big enough. Why don't we do two sessions? Bethy and I can go first." Conrad extracts his arm from behind Bethy and gets to his feet. He holds a hand out to her. "The attic and second floor?"

"Sounds good." Mason looks to Nat. "Are you participating? You can do your thing with the ghosts."

She hesitates for a second. "I guess."

"Why don't you take the cellar? Maybe you can settle whatever spirit is riled up down there."

"Great. I get to go into the rain." Nat gives Mason a look I can't decipher. "Don't be a fool while I'm gone."

He shoots her a saucy grin that promises mischief. The flashlight lights up the planes of his face, turning him into a spooky clown. The three of them—Nat, Conrad, and Bethy—leave the room.

The front door closes behind Nat. I don't think any of us should go into the cellar. It gave me the chills, but Nat can handle herself. I shouldn't worry about her. I say nothing about how frightening the cellar is in case it gives Mason any ideas about where he should send me for my solo mission. Even the attic is preferable, though not by much.

Above us, Bethy and Conrad's footsteps make the floorboards creak. Their voices drift down the stairs, words inaudible.

"To your places, guys!" Mason yells towards the ceiling. There's muffled laughter and the sound of footsteps retreating further up the stairs, presumably to the attic.

Silence falls around Mason and me like an uncomfortable blanket. I don't know him well enough to make meaningful conversation, nor am I comfortable with the house. I don't want to talk about the weather when there could be a spirit in the room plotting our deaths. And I want to be respectful of what we're doing, to those we're trying to put to rest. So I stay silent. Mason doesn't let me worry about the silence for long. He breaks it by asking, "Are you having fun?"

I blink a few times, not sure how to answer that. "I guess. It's been pretty scary."

"Do you think you'll join us on another hunt?" His voice is hopeful. He isn't looking right at me, but off to the side, which gives his question weight. He wants me to say yes. That realization warms me. My presence is wanted.

I shrug, leaning against the soft pillows of the couch. "Probably. Nat's pretty cool. I think I could learn a lot from her."

"The rest of us could teach you too."

"Maybe."

He scoots forward in his seat, leans his elbows on his knees, and looks at me with intent eyes. The flashlight, set so the bulb faces the ceiling, lights him up so that his eyes practically glow. "Riley, I want to ask you something..."

CHAPTER ELEVEN

Hanna:
1817-1833

My necklace gleams in the silvery moonlight. Mama told me to hide it, to not let anyone know I had it. It had been her mother's before it was hers. Grandmama had given it to Mama when Mama was sold. Mama said it was a gift from the white man who had fathered her. She said he and Grandmama had loved each other, but I couldn't see how that was possible. How could you love those who held you captive and took your children from you? Still, it is my treasure, because the two women before me loved it. It is my only tie to them.

The door to the attic creaks open. Heavy footsteps thud up the stairs. Fear permeates the room. The other girls who are not asleep fall still, silencing their breaths. He mustn't know they're awake. He might choose them.

Quickly, I tuck my necklace into the neck of my tattered nightgown. The fabric is stained yellow with age, others having used it before me. I huddle into my narrow cot, pulling the thin blanket over my shoulders. It is too hot for blankets. But I don't want to be exposed. I want to be invisible.

I clamp my eyes shut and pretend to sleep.

His footsteps march down the narrow aisle between the two rows of sleeping girls.

I hold my breath as the steps pause near the foot of my cot. I'm still new here, and young, and the eldest Turner son has a reputation for breaking in the new girls. I crack an eyelid, needing to know if his interest is on me.

The moonlight makes him pale as a ghost. The whites of his eyes glint as he watches me. I bite the inside of my lip to keep from making a sound. He must think me dead asleep.

Thankfully, he moves on. Cotton rustles as he shakes someone awake across the aisle. There is a moan—Betty. He shushes her. Then the sound of his boots retreats through the attic, followed by the slap of Betty's bare feet on the floorboards.

Through my nightgown, I clench my necklace. If he comes for me next and finds this, they will accuse me of theft. The punishment I could withstand, but not the loss of the necklace.

I must be quick; hide it before they return. I rise from my cot and peer about the attic. There are so many of us. I have to hide it somewhere I can get it quick, but somewhere safe, where another girl won't find it. I pad to the end of the attic, next to Betty's cot.

I kneel, feeling the floorboards. There is a small crack between the boards and the wall. I pry the board up with calloused fingers, then slide the necklace into the small hole. It's not perfect, but it's safer here than around my neck. I will return for it one day, when it's safe. I pat the floorboard.

Hopefully, I will return for it soon.

......

Present Day

"I really like you," Mason says.

Oh no... I don't like his tone of voice. I rub my hands on my pants, swallowing hard.

"Do you think—"

"That's so nice of you!" I cut him off with a false, bubbly voice. I sound like one of those preppy girls from my old school, the kind of girl I thought Bethy was, until I got to know her. I clear my throat and continue. "I think you guys are great, too. It's so nice to make friends my age in Salvation Hills, you know? You, Conrad, and Bethy are really cool." I don't mention Nat. Somehow, I can't group her in with my other new friends. A mentor maybe? But that title doesn't really fit either.

He lets my words soak in for a few seconds. When he speaks, he says the word like it's new to him. "Friends. Yeah. We're good friends."

He seems hurt. But I can't start something with Mason. He is really not my type. Attractive, sure. But tonight's teaching me he can be pretty selfish and single-minded. Besides, I'm living a lie, so I can't have a real relationship, anyway. It's better that Mason and I remain friends. Uncomfortable, I rub my hands on my pants again, then cross my arms over my chest to keep from fidgeting.

"Can we come down now?" Conrad calls from the top of the stairs. I don't know how long they've been up there, but it's been a while.

Mason looks at his watch, his back straight and his face pointedly turned away from me. He answers sullenly. "Yeah. Time's up."

Conrad retreats down the hall and bangs on a door. There's the creaking of hinges, then his voice calling, "Bethy, time's up."

The front door opens and Nat calls, "I'm back."

She stomps her feet on the entry mat a few times, then walks into the living room. Rain dots her clothes, and her hair is damp. She rubs her hands together and looks from me to Mason. "What? Am I early?"

As she says this, Bethy and Conrad come down the stairs, hand-in-hand. In seconds, Bethy's taken the two of us in. I can only imagine what she sees. Me, arms crossed over my chest, scrunched up on the far corner of the couch, and Mason, with his sad, puppy-dog eyes and dejected expression. Who'd have thought telling someone they were your friend could make them look so sad?

"Did something happen?" Conrad asks.

Bethy bursts out laughing and flops onto the couch beside me. "Mason, you're such an idiot. You don't need to tell every girl you love them."

Every girl, huh? If he's done this before, I don't feel so bad.

Conrad's expression lightens. He slaps Mason on the shoulder as he passes. "You need to read the room. Riley isn't interested in you." He sits beside Bethy on the couch.

Nat falls back into the armchair, swings one leg over the other, and looks from me to Mason. "It's your turn to go solo."

"It's always Mason's turn going solo," Bethy laughs.

That seems harsh. Suddenly, I feel sorry for him. I know what it's like to be alone.

"Ha ha," Mason says hollowly, then immediately perks up. "I call the second-floor where I saw the apparition!"

"Why? You almost peed yourself last time." Conrad looks at him appraisingly. "Trying to prove you're not a chicken?"

Mason flips Conrad off. "I'm prepared this time."

"Uh-huh."

"Why don't you go back to the attic, Riley?" Nat suggests. "It's probably better for you than the cellar."

I nod, wanting to ask what happened to her in the cellar that would encourage her to send me to the attic, where a ghost tried to throw me down the stairs. Then I decide I don't want to know right before I go on my solo.

I follow Mason upstairs. As soon as we're away from the others, he falls silent. I may have turned down his advances, but why is he acting like an ass? I tried to be nice about it. I don't want to give him false hope, especially if I come ghost hunting with them again. If he even invites me, now. I don't want him to hate me, but I don't want to lead him on, either.

We reach the second-floor landing. Mason gestures down the hall. "I'll take Eric's room. You're okay upstairs?"

I nod, glad he's able to talk to me. Maybe he'll get over it. He hands me a camera and pushes the record button. I wonder if his confession and my rejection were recorded. Would Bethy put that in the final cut of the video? It's not embarrassing for me, but I doubt Mason would take it well. People can be mean in the comments and he seems pretty touchy.

"You know what to do?" he asks.

"I've seen your videos." I'm dreading the little door and the dark, narrow stairs. It'll be scary with no flashlight, but I have my phone. If I get truly desperate, I have thirty percent battery and the flashlight function.

"See you in ten," Mason says, his voice still monotone. He wants me to know he's upset.

I take a deep breath as I open the door to the attic and step into the darkness. At least on the second floor there's a bit of light; not much, but just enough to give one hope. Not like this solid black darkness. But I can do this. It's ten minutes alone in the dark. I sleep in my car, for crying out loud. Well, I used to sleep in my car. I might not be sleeping in it anymore. That's a worry for another time.

The stairs are just as narrow as I remember. I keep my hand on the wall and take each step one at a time. The entire house seems alive up here, sighing and breathing with every gust of wind. The old wood shifts and groans below me, as though complaining about the storm.

Once I reach the top of the stairs, I tiptoe to the centre of the room. I'd planned to sit down and meditate, keep my mind off the ghosts. We're not supposed to stir anything up, so I don't even want to talk to myself, in case a spirit takes offense to that. But it's too quiet and creepy. I don't like the groaning and creaking of the rafters. My skin crawls as though I'm being watched, so I pace the room.

I say nothing, just walk from one side to the other. It's hard not to imagine all the people who would have slept up here. I wonder if they were resigned to it or if they yearned for somewhere else. No matter who they were, I bet they wanted to go home, to be with their families. My chest is tight, and tears prick at my eyes. It isn't right to tear people apart.

The floorboards creak underfoot. At the end of the attic I stub my toes on the pile of boxes stacked there. I wonder if these boxes came with the house or if the Lees put them here. It's strange to place them at the very back of the attic when nothing else is up here, but maybe they had plans for this space.

The small window on this wall is dusty, the yard below hidden by the night. I jump when a bolt of lightning zigzags across the sky. Turning, I blink away the afterimage, and thunder shakes the house. Another flash lights up the attic. Something twinkles behind the boxes at the base of the wall.

I kneel on the hard floor and feel around. The floor is dusty. Fly bodies litter the crack between the boxes and the wall. I aim the camera at the spot, hoping to see another glimmer of light. It was probably just a nail. But why was it shiny?

Another bolt of lightning illuminates the room. Again, something sparkles. I reach out as the subsequent crash of thunder rattles the window.

There's a small crack between the floorboard and the wall. In this space, I can feel what might be a thin chain. I use my nail to try to catch it. Could it be a necklace? And if so, whose? How did it get up here?

I lean against the wall to get a better angle. My fingernail lifts a loop of the chain and my finger slides under it. I tug gently, not wanting to break it, but it's stuck between the wall and floorboards. I lean harder against the wall, trying to budge the panel.

Another flash lights up the window, casting the attic in shades of gray. The necklace comes loose and the wall beside me gives way. For a split second, I am suspended in open air, arms flailing. My fingers scrabble for grip, but there is none. I plummet into darkness. The wall panel bangs into place above me. Thunder shakes the house, drowning out my scream.

I slam onto the ground, feet first. Pain shoots up my legs. I tumble out of the wall, sprawling on cold, hard dirt. The air is knocked out of me. I struggle to catch my breath. Everything hurts, but I can move my arms and legs. I'm lucky I'm not dead.

I sit up, cracking my head on something cold and hard. Tenderly, I cover the spot with my hand. It's pulsing and hot. I can't tell if it's bleeding, but it's most likely a good goose-egg. What did I hit? I reach out, and my fingers brush against a rough stone pillar. Where am I?

I need light. I pat the ground, searching for my phone or the camera. They fell with me, so they must be here. But there's nothing around me but dirt. I shudder. Am I in the cellar? Could I have fallen that far? Slowly, I take a deep, even breath to combat the panic overwhelming my rational thoughts. I need to find a light source so I can find my way out of here. I *need* to get out.

After several deep breaths that don't calm me, I rock forward so I can feel the stone column or arch I hit my head on. My fingers drift down it. It's rough and old, like the stone the cistern room was made of. My breath flutters, my heart racing. I don't want to be in the cellar. The cistern was almost full—what if I drown down here? I listen for trickling water and hear none. The dirt is dry beneath my fingers. I'm probably safe from drowning. I can only deal with one threat at a time. And this is definitely the cellar.

From the pillar, which is the best landmark I have, I splay my hands on the ground and feel around, inch by inch, so I miss nothing. Nothing but dried clumps of dirt and rocks. What can I do? How will the others ever find me? I hug my knees to my chest and press my face against them, my breath coming in shallow gasps as I fight back panic. I need to get out. The house presses in above me. It's like a grave down here. I don't want to die alone, under a haunted house.

A scraping sound comes from my left. I freeze, listening to it draw nearer. It's definitely coming towards me. I scream and scramble away, but my back hits the wall. I bring my arms up to shield my face. What is it? A rat? Is it still coming at me? Something presses against the edge of my shoe. I scream again.

"Your phone," Riley whispers. I jump, but I don't scream. I'm getting used to her popping out of nowhere.

I reach down, my fingers trembling until they graze the smooth screen of my phone. I hug it to my chest, but only for a second. The next moment I'm entering my passcode with dirt covered hands. The screen lights up. There's a crack across the upper right-hand side, but otherwise it seems fine. It has power and unlocks without a problem. I press the flashlight icon and the small space I'm in is flooded with bright, white light.

I squint from the brightness, blinking until my eyes adjust. The camera is a few feet away. I crawl over to it and pick it up. It's dead. I hope it's not broken. There's a glitter in the dirt by my feet—the necklace. I fish it free and shove it in my pocket. Riley sits across from me, cross-legged.

"Where have you been?" I ask angrily. "You left me."

She shrugs. *"The others don't like strangers, including me. I've been lurking. I wouldn't leave you. Where would I go?"*

She glances around our dirt prison, her brow furrowing. Her cadence changes, becomes jerky and stilted. *"I can't. Stay long. He's coming. He likes you. You're easy."*

My skin prickles. "Who's he?"

Riley doesn't talk like this. I don't like it. It's too ghostly and creepy.

She shrugs. *"The one. In charge."*

I pan the room with my light. I'm below the house, but not the same part of the cellar we'd been in before. This part is shallow, the ceiling only three feet above the dirt floors. Over my head are support beams and old floorboards. The foundation seems to be built on stone walls that meet in a corner behind me. In the distance, they criss-cross the foundation. Stone support columns rise out of the dirt like blunt teeth, casting the crawl space beyond them in darkness. I'm boxed in. There's no way out.

"How do I get out?" I ask. Hopefully, Riley has an answer. She can go places I can't.

"Climb up the way you came?" She peers into the darkness over our heads, seeming more like herself. I crawl over, careful not to bump my pounding head again. A narrow chute extends up into dark. There's nothing I could grab onto if I were to try climbing up.

"I'll call Mason." My phone battery has dropped to twenty percent in the short time I've been using the flashlight. I find Mason's name in my contacts and push call, but nothing happens. I try again, but with the same result.

"Maybe the storm?" Riley leans over to look at the screen and the battery icon immediately turns red. Fifteen percent. I'd been at nearly thirty before I fell.

"Riley, you're draining my battery!" I yell, holding my phone away from her.

She looks at me with sad eyes. *"I'm sorry. I was trying to help."*

"Never mind. I'll text the group before my phone dies." I turn my attention to the screen, my fingers flying over the keyboard: *Fell into crawl space under house. Can't get out.*

I push send. A few moments later, my phone chimes. I have no signal and the message failed. The flashlight turns off. A low battery notification fills my screen.

"I guess that's it," I say to Riley. When I look up, turning my screen to light up the space, she's gone. I shouldn't have yelled at her. She was trying to help.

Suddenly, the crawl space is freezing cold. I wrap my arms around myself, my teeth chattering. I scan the darkness. An ethereal green mist floats across my vision. I rub my eyes, sure that I'm imagining things, or maybe it's just so dark that I'm seeing lights that aren't there. But no; these are the remaining spirits in the house. Fear settles on me. I shake, either from the cold or the fear, I can't tell. A tendril of air brushes my ear. A ghostly whisper. The words indiscernible, the voice distinctly male. I shuffle away from it, hunching in on myself.

The whisper comes again. I clamp my eyes shut. I can't see anything, anyway.

"Go away," I mutter through clenched teeth.

A weight drapes across my back like an arm. I don't feel comforted. The voice whispers again. This time I can make out the hissed words, *"No. You go away."*

Nat said that fear feeds them. I refuse to feed them, though I'm quaking on my haunches. I keep my eyes closed and pretend I'm anywhere but here. It doesn't work. Why did I think this hunt was a good idea?

"Get out," the voice says again, thick with rage. *"Get out of my house!"*

I can't help it. His anger is too strong. Shaking with terror, I crawl forward along the foundation, trying to find any space big enough to climb through. The rage of the spirit follows me, growing stronger. But I'm trying. I'm trying.

My hand brushes something hard and smooth, topped with fluff. I push it aside, but it's attached to something else. My hand slips and my thumb sinks into a hole. I recoil, knowing innately what I've just touched.

Ghost forgotten, I click on my phone screen with trembling hands and turn it around. In the dim light, the smooth, curved bone is pale, the vacant eye sockets dark. A tuft of brown hair falls across the forehead. The skull is tilted towards me, the jaw gaping in a toothy grin. The rest of the skeleton extends back into the darkness, scraps of clothing clinging to bone.

I shuffle back, away from the awful sight. My phone goes dark. I press the side button again. Nothing. The battery is dead. My heart pounds in my ears. I whimper, pressing backwards until my back hits the wall. I curl up, my hands over my head, quivering with fear. I'm going to die down here.

Chapter Twelve

Jason Glinsmann:
1982-2010

The sun is setting, casting everything in gold. This is a nice neighbourhood, very quiet. Not a lot of nosy neighbours. In the week I've been visiting the place, no one has noticed me. I turn the corner and approach the end of the street. My heavy backpack weighs me down. I've shoved it full of all my possessions, hoping my house will still be empty.

There it is. Dark against the sky, nestled back among the trees like a chick in a nest. It's perfect. The driveway is empty and the windows gleam golden from the sun, but the house itself is dark. I'm sure it feels sad sitting empty. I'll give it purpose again.

I look over my shoulder, but the street is quiet. Like a shadow, I duck into the trees and make my way around to the back. The lock on the back door is easily picked. I enter the house before night has fully settled on the world.

I step into the kitchen, flashlight in hand, my footsteps echoing through the empty house. Someone's done renovations. The countertops in here are definitely new, as are the floors. I drop off my backpack in the utility room and unlatch the window. If someone shows up, I'll need to take off in short order. I don't need to use the entire house, anyway. Just this room will be fine. I'm still going to explore the rest of this place, though.

I tiptoe through the house, keeping my light directed at the floor. There are no curtains and I don't want to tip off any neighbours that I've moved in. I head carefully up the dark stairs. All the bedrooms are empty. It looks like no one is living here right now. The utility room will work just fine then. Parts of the house have been modernized, but whoever did the renovations kept a lot of historical charm. I can practically hear the voices of previous occupants.

I freeze, listening. There *are* voices whispering in this place.

"Hello," I say to the spirits of the house. "I've come to join you for a while."

I step to the window at the end of the hall and lean against the wall as I peer out. Part of the paneling shifts under my weight. I jump back, hoping I haven't damaged this grand house. No—there's a small knob, the same colour as the wall. This is a door.

Narrow steps lead up to a dark attic with a sloped ceiling, dusty floors. No one has been up here for a long time. This might be a nice place to stay, too. If there's a second access panel, I might consider bringing my stuff up here. It would give me a great view of the yard and allow me to stay hidden if the owner comes back. I cross to the other side of the attic and search that wall for another hidden panel.

A cool breeze brushes my face. I turn, searching for the source, feeling a sudden surge of sadness. There's no one there. I blink away tears, about to turn back to my search, when a voice whispers from across the attic. Disembodied voices are nothing new to me. They've been my companions for years.

I clear my throat and say, "What was that? I couldn't quite make it out."

"*Then join us!*" the voice says, clear as day.

A powerful force rushes me, throwing me back against the wall. Something gives, and I'm falling. Pain slices through my arm. I land hard, tumble forward, and smash my face against rock.

I pull myself to my knees with a groan, but hit my head as soon as I sit up. Lying down, I feel around. Dirt, rock, debris. There—my flashlight. I turn it on, relieved when the beam flickers and comes on. Once I see what the light illuminates, my relief vanishes. I'm in a tight space, presumably beneath the house. I know I was in the attic, but I don't know how I fell. The light plays over the floorboards above me. I press on each one, trying to loosen them. They don't budge.

My arm is bleeding heavily. I take off my T-shirt, pressing it against the gash, but that doesn't help. If I can get out, a neighbour could call for help. I drag myself across the dirt. If there's a crawlspace, there's got to be access to it.

There's nothing. Nothing I can find, at least. Weariness consumes me. I'll take a small nap. Maybe when I wake, I'll see it. I'm probably missing it because of the shock. I lie back, using a clod of dirt to cushion my head. What will my parents think if I die down here? I hope they miss me. I hope someone misses me.

········

Present Day

I'm trapped in the house's underbelly. With a skeleton, no less. Darkness presses in, thick with spirits. Invisible hands claw at me, drawn to my fear. My heart pounds. My breath comes in gasps until I can bear it no more. I scream.

My heart is racing in my chest, pulse pounding in my ears. Distantly, there's the rush of wind, the crashing of a tree, and, faintly, the shouting of voices. I gasp for air, unable to bear the murmuring of the ghosts. Tears stream down my face.

A distant voice calls out, "Riley!"

Yes. I need Riley. I need my best friend.

Is this how she felt? Before she died? Was she this tormented and anguished, bullied by her peers and neglected by the people who were supposed to take care of her?

Why didn't she tell me? I knew she was unhappy. I thought I was too. Typical teenage stuff, like curfews and school. We could have dealt with it together. Run away or something. We could have been here, in Salvation Hills, together. Rented a small apartment together and started our own lives. I could have saved her. Instead, she gave up.

My fear dissolves, leaving only guilt and grief. I bury my face in my dirty hands and sob. The dam I'd built to keep my pain from touching me is gone. Riley, my best friend, has left this world forever. We didn't graduate together. We won't ever get an apartment together, or go to the same college. Or even talk about our latest crush or favourite fashion, not ever again. I have to do those things on my own. Or, with new friends. But I don't want to leave her behind.

Eventually, my sobs fade to hiccups. I'm dry, physically and emotionally. My head aches, my eyes are swollen, my throat raw, but I am more myself, more at peace than I have been since I first learned that Riley was gone.

"Riley!" The shouts come again, this time not drowned out by my sorrowful sobs. I sit up and rub my dirty hands over my tear-streaked face.

"I'm here! Under the house." My voice is muffled by the wind and soft dirt floor. What time is it now? It must be nearly dawn. Maybe when the sun rises, they'll be able to find a way to me.

I feel around in the dirt, careful to avoid the bones, until I find a decent-sized rock. I use it to hit the floor above me, hoping the sound will carry over the storm. Will they have to tear the floor up to get to me? How embarrassing would that be? But I need to get out. What if they never find me? I'll become just another spirit haunting the place. At least Riley and I would be together again.

But I don't want to die. I'm not Riley. I want to be Lanie again. I bang harder against the floor.

I swear the voices pause, as though listening, then footsteps creak the floorboards nearby. I hit the floor, then yell. "I'm here. Below the house!"

Someone knocks on the floor. "Riley?"

"Yes! It's me." I tap the floor again, relief and excitement coursing through me.

"You guys, I found her." Though muffled, the voice clearly belongs to Bethy.

More footsteps thunder above me. The low rumble of voices filters through the floor.

"Riley?" Mason shouts down to me. I imagine him facedown on the floor, yelling through cupped hands. "We'll get you out of there. The storm's almost over and the sun should be up soon. Don't worry."

I sink against the wall, at peace for the first time since falling down here. Who cares about spiders, snakes, or ghosts? I've finally come to some sort of peace with Riley's death. And I think I've made new friends.

I close my eyes, listening to the murmur of voices above me. There are spirits lingering nearby. I can feel them, but I'm not scared. I'm not giving them any more power. I lean my head against the wall and drift into dreams where I'm hunting ghosts in my childhood home. My parents don't like it. They think ghosts are evil, but Riley and I don't care. We're having too much fun.

·········

"Lanie, wake up."

Riley is with me when I open my eyes, faintly visible in the darkness. Then I realize it's not so dark down here. I can see the outline of things. Like the shape of the skull. Goodie.

"The sun's coming up," Riley says.

Instead of looking for a way out, I stare at Riley for a long moment, taking in her familiar features. "I can't believe you're gone. Why did you leave me?"

Her dark eyes blink at me, moist with tears. *"I didn't mean to leave you, but I just couldn't bear it anymore. You were the only person who cared about me."*

"And now I'm suffering. I wish you would have told me. I would have done anything for you."

"I didn't know how. I'm sorry. I promise I won't ever leave you again."

That doesn't seem healthy, but I'm not about to contradict her. I want her to stay, too. Plus, I don't want to reject her. She had enough of that when she was alive. "I miss you."

"I miss you too, but let's get you out of here before that angry man comes back. He wants to hurt you."

I shudder. "Where did he go?"

She touches my shoulder, urging me to crawl towards the distant speck of light. *"Who knows? He thinks this is his house and resents the living for being here."*

"Did he live here?" Mason knows the history of the house. He'll probably figure out who the guy was. Maybe he's the one Nat's been sensing. She seemed afraid of him. Riley's right. I need to get out before he comes back.

"Duh. Now move it."

Riley's answer is so her that I have to remind myself she's gone. Tears prick at my eyes, but the grief is a dull ache now, no longer all-consuming.

I crawl towards the light. There's a small space where the stone support doesn't quite reach the wooden beam above it. It's barely wide enough for me to squeeze through. The stone catches my sleeves on either side as I do. The light gets bigger, brighter as I get closer, though I still can't make out where it's coming from. Ahead of me is another stone wall. I poke my head above this. The space beyond the stones is dim, filled with a gentle tinkle of water. I can just make out the hulking shape of the rusted water heater and the familiar sagging steps of the cellar. Bright daylight shines in through the open cellar door.

It takes some maneuvering—and hyperventilating when I get wedged between the rocks and the floor—but soon I'm over the wall and dropping to the cellar floor, exhausted. I'd like nothing more than to lie down and get a good sleep, but I need to get away from the murderous ghost first.

I run to the steps. The cellar doors were never padlocked when we left. One side is open, probably the wind's doing, and early morning light streams in. At some point during the night the storm had blown over, though the sky is still studded with gray clouds. I step onto the stairs, towards the light, joy pulsing through my veins.

The door slams shut.

I jump, nearly falling off the stairs. Wind, that's all. I race up the remaining steps and push on the doors. They hold firm, as though locked. A thin seam of morning light shines between them, but otherwise, the cellar is as dark as it had been the night before.

I bang on the doors. "Hey, let me out!"

Behind me, someone chuckles. The hairs on the back of my neck prickle. Slowly, I turn. A man stands in the centre of the dirt floor, head down, eyes glaring up at me from under bushy eyebrows. He's pale, almost see-through. Faint, green light emanates from him, shifting like mist.

He's a tall man, over six feet. His head would brush the floorboards above if he were corporeal. His beard hangs down his chest, straggly and yellow. Most terrifying, outside of the fact that he's semi-transparent, are his eyes. They're entirely black, pupils and irises blown so wide there are no whites. The room reeks of body odor and stale pipe smoke. Trembling, I step back before I remember that ghosts feed off emotions. This guy doesn't look like he needs anymore feeding. He's plenty powerful. It radiates off him.

He steps towards me. I stand up straighter and fist my hands at my sides. How do you defend yourself against a manifesting, angry ghost? I muster all my strength and channel it in my voice. "Stay away from me!"

I think the ghost smiles, but it looks like a grimace. The corner of his mouth twitches up, but his bushy gray eyebrows narrow over his black eyes.

"I told you. To get out." His voice is a growl. Goosebumps slither across my arms.

I summon my best Riley impression and defiantly jut out my chin. "Open the door and I will."

Slowly, he shakes his head. *"Too late."*

He rushes me. He's so fast he loses physical shape, roaring forwards and reappearing inches from me. Ghostly hands wrap around my neck. His mouth opens in a toothless scream of rage. I scrabble at his hold, to no avail. My hands go right through him.

He flings me across the room. I narrowly miss the water heater, and land in a sprawl against the lip of the cistern. Heavy footsteps thump towards me, leaving no impression in the dirt. I look up at the ghost man. I can't physically overpower him. How do I fight a ghost?

Maybe reason will work.

My throat aches, bruised by phantom hands. I rasp out, "It's hard with so many people in your space. Let me go, and I'll tell them to leave. Please let me go."

He stops, his boots inches away. *"Not good enough. They always return. Always."*

He bends down, outstretched fingers reaching for my neck. I have nowhere to go. Nothing to do. I flinch away as his icy touch grazes my skin.

A familiar, banshee-like scream splits the air and Riley materializes from nowhere, launching herself at the man. She collides with him, arms outstretched, and wraps herself around him. He staggers back, arms flailing, beating at her back. She grunts, but holds on, her face contorting with effort. The man screams as Riley presses herself tighter, her body moulding to his.

She looks at me over his shoulder. *"Get out of here."*

I roll onto my knees and stand on shaky legs. Both ghosts screech, ear-rattling, inhuman cries. The cellar grows hot, then icy cold. A popping, sizzling sound fills the room. Riley begins to glow, candescent green radiating off her until she's blazing with it. Suddenly, they flash out of sight, as quickly as a TV clicking off.

"Riley?" I call. No answer.

The Riley-shaped hole in my heart aches. I don't know what she did, but I hope she's okay.

I limp towards the cellar stairs and wobble up them. I take a deep breath, praying the doors will open. With all my remaining strength, I fling them wide. A gust of fresh morning air washes over me as the doors slam against the house, nearly hitting Mason in the face.

He yelps and falls back.

"Riley?" Bethy rushes forward. "Are you okay? We heard screaming."

The dark hole behind me is empty and serene.

"There was a ghost. An old white guy." I let Bethy pull me up the last step and out onto the grass.

"Really?" Mason leans towards the dark entry, then shoots me a shrewd look. "How did you know he was old?"

"She saw him, Mase." Nat puts an arm around my shoulders, disregarding my dirt-crusted clothes. She smooths a strand of my hair behind my ear. "Are you sure you're all right?"

I shake my head, my throat tight with emotion. "It was Riley who saved me. I don't—she might have crossed over."

A frown creases Nat's forehead. "No, I don't think she did. Nor did the other ghost, the one who was hiding from me. I can still feel him, though whatever she did weakened him."

I stare at Nat. Where did Riley go if she didn't cross over? "Will she come back to me?"

Nat's arm tightens around my shoulders. "She'll come back when she's ready."

Mason's glaring at me. "Riley? What do you mean, *Riley* saved you? Who is she? Who are *you*?"

I heave a sigh. "It's a long story. Can we sit down?"

Chapter Thirteen

The power is still out and probably will be for a few days. At least until the downed trees are cleared. So we sit on the verandah where the morning sun slowly soaks into me, warm and comforting. But it can't compete with the warmth of Nat sitting beside me with her arm over my shoulders, or the gentle press of Bethy sitting at my feet, leaning up against my legs. Whatever else happened tonight, the best part was making new friends.

"My name isn't Riley Miller. It's Lanie Gilbert." I give them my story as bare-bones as I can, leaving out as much emotion as possible, though I still tear up in parts. I also don't tell them I'm living in my car. It's pretty obvious, but I don't need more pity. "I'm really sorry I lied to everyone about who I am. I guess I was trying to hold on to Riley as long as possible."

Nat gives my shoulders a squeeze. "You only lied about your name. You didn't lie about who you are."

"I pretended to be Riley. She was always the brave one. I'm not as fearless as she is."

Conrad chuckles, pressing his foot against the floorboards to get the porch swing to move. "You were trapped in a crawl space in the cellar for over three hours, haunted by ghosts and nearly killed by one, but you walked out of there by yourself with your sanity intact. I'd say you're pretty brave."

"You have all the luck," Mason whines. "You can see ghosts, you have a tragic backstory, and you have a ghost best friend. I can't even get proper evidence that ghosts exist on camera. You're not leaving our group."

"Do you think you'll join us for another hunt?" Bethy asks.

Before I can answer, my stomach rumbles. I clamp my hands over it, my cheeks burning.

Bethy laughs. "Will you come if we promise to feed you next time?"

At that moment, a car horn beeps and the Lee's van pulls across the end of the driveway. They can't get in because of the downed tree. Mr. and Mrs. Lee get out of the vehicle and take in the fallen tree before they look at the house. As far as I know, there's no storm damage to the exterior of the house, and only a bit of ghost damage inside.

Mrs. Lee holds up a paper bag as she and Mr. Lee walk around the tree and across the lawn. "Hungry? We brought breakfast. The storm was awful where we were, so we couldn't help but come home early to check on the house. We left the kids with my parents."

"Let me help you with that." Mason jumps down the front steps and hurries to take the bag from her. "Ooh, it's still hot. Great. The power's out."

The Lees join us on the verandah for breakfast sandwiches and coffee while we tell them about last night. Mrs. Lee nods along with what we tell her, seeming unsurprised. Mr. Lee remains completely still until we finish giving him a rundown of all the ghostly activity, including the discovery of potential murder weapons. I leave out any mention of Riley. She's my personal ghost.

When we're done, Mr. Lee rubs his face.

"What can we do? We can't let the kids grow up in a haunted house," he says with a sigh.

"Blessing the house and cleansing it will help," Nat suggests. "I can recommend someone. And you can set an intention for the negative spirits to leave and the peaceful ones to stay, if you wish."

"Will that be enough?" Mrs. Lee asks.

"It should be. The angry man is just a human spirit who thinks he owns the place. But it's your home now. You can claim it and send him packing. Or you could lay down some ground rules if you want to let him stay, but based on how he's controlling the other spirits, I think he should go." Nat takes a long swallow of coffee. She looks tired, pale with dark bags under her eyes. I guess after thirty, you feel all-nighters more.

I hesitate before speaking, but the Lees need to know this. "There's something else. While I was in the crawl space, I found something you won't be too happy about."

"What?" Mr. Lee asks, an edge of caution in his voice.

I swallow. "There were bones down there. Human bones."

Mrs. Lee makes a little cry, her hands flying up to cover her mouth.

Mr. Lee pats her knee, and leans forward to ask, "Are you sure?"

I nod. "They were unmistakable."

Mrs. Lee grabs her husband's hand. "The missing squatter."

Mr. Lee nods. "We need to call the police."

······•·•····

While we wait for the police, Mr. Lee gets out a chainsaw and starts cutting the branches off the tree that fell over the driveway. Once those are hauled aside, it's obvious that my poor car has seen better days. The windshield has a jagged crack running across it and one passenger-side window has completely shattered where a branch broke through. The backseat, and most of my belongings, are soaked.

Nat's motorcycle is parked where she left it, surrounded by fallen branches, completely unscathed.

I'm standing beside my car, staring at it in dismay, when Nat comes up and bumps my hip with hers. I say nothing. The only words that would come out are: what do I do now? I don't want to be that pathetic. Not in front of Nat.

"I'm sorry about your car. You know, I have an extra room. Any chance you'd like to stay with me for a while?"

"How'd you know?" I ask, my voice thick.

She gestures at the toothbrush and pillow in the backseat. "It's pretty obvious. Plus, Conrad told me. Do you need to think about it?"

I shake my head, sniffling, and grab her in a tight hug. A safe place to stay while I get my home fixed up is just what I need. That and a few hours of sleep after an intense night. I won't get that for a while, though. I shove my hands in my pockets with a sigh, only to feel something solid. I pull it out—the necklace.

"This is what I was trying to get when I fell into the cellar." I give Nat the necklace. "It was caught under a floorboard in the attic. Good thing I remembered. I should probably give it to the Lees."

She raises an eyebrow as she turns it over in her hand. "You could give it to them. It technically came with the house, but it belonged to the girl who was in the attic."

"Was she wearing it?"

Nat shakes her head. "No, but I can sense it. It was special to her."

She returns it to me. I shove it back in my pocket, though that feels sacrilegious now.

"Hey, guys," Bethy calls from the treeline off to the side of the house. Mason and Conrad are already with her. "Come over here for a second."

"What is it?" Nat asks when we get close enough to speak in normal tones.

"Riley—I mean, Lanie, where did you see the guy in the trees?" She twists her hands nervously.

I'd almost forgotten about seeing the man last night. I think back, considering. "It was about right here."

Bethy nods. "I think so too. Look." She steps into the trees, pointing. "There's a path here. It's covered with debris from the storm, but it leads towards the neighbour's house. Do you think the man might not have been a ghost? I'm not a psychic and I saw him."

"I didn't see him," Nat says. "I thought then that he might've been living."

"Hear me out, guys." Mason holds out his hands, his eyes glinting with excitement. "What if it was the Salvation Hills 'Napper?"

"The what?" Bethy steps out of the trees.

"I just made that name up," Mason admits. "But it could have been him! The guy who kidnapped that missing woman."

"You're jumping to conclusions again, Mase," Conrad says. "First, we don't know who kidnapped her, or if anyone did. Second, there might not have been a man out here last night. We didn't all see it."

"Fine, but I'm sticking to my theory. I was right about the squatter."

Before Mason can think of more theories, the police arrive. They've been busy with downed power lines and people in more immediate distress after the storm. I lead them and Mr. Lee, who wants to see the bones for himself, down into the cellar. The officers are both big men, neither of them nor Mr. Lee, are small enough to fit through the gap I had to crawl through. There doesn't seem to be a better way in, so I take their camera and crawl back into the dark, dirty crawlspace.

Something cold brushes against me as I dip below a wooden beam, and the rough wood catches the back of my shirt. A cruel voice whispers in my ear, but I ignore him. This ghost has no power over me. My fear is no longer in control. I won't let him affect me.

When I reach the bones, I don't touch them. The officers instructed me not to, though I told them I'd already run into them in the dark. They don't want me to disturb the scene any more than I already have; they just need proof that there's something amiss before they deconstruct the Lees' cellar.

I snap a few pictures, the flash of the camera reflecting off exposed bone. My heart is heavy at the fear and loneliness this guy must have felt, knowing he was going to die down here with nobody ever knowing what had happened to him. The skeleton can't be that old. Clothes still cover it. The way the jaw hangs open and one hand sprawls over the skull makes him look so vulnerable. How had he ended up here? What had he been running from? Whatever it was, this must have been a horrible way to go.

"Are you going to get me out of here?" A soft, male voice asks.

I look past the bones to where a man squats, cheeks hollow and pale, thin brown hair wisping over his forehead. I swallow back the lump that forms in my throat.

"This is you?" I point at the bones. He nods, sadly.

"We'll get you out and lay you to rest. Are you Jason Glinsmann?"

He nods again. *"How did you know?"*

"Your parents have been looking for you. There are theories you were squatting here before you disappeared."

"I was. But the man trapped me down here. Get me out?"

Before I can answer, he fades away, as though he's used all his energy.

I crawl back to the crack of light and pass the camera through before I maneuver myself out of the crawlspace. I hope I never have to go back in there.

Mason, Bethy, Conrad and Nat are sitting on the cellar steps, watching with curious and concerned eyes. I join them, the steps shifting under my weight.

The officers raise their eyebrows when they look at the pictures I've taken. Mr. Lee looks over their shoulders, then turns away, running a hand through his hair, his eyes strained.

"It's Jason Glinsmann," I whisper to the others.

"Really?" Mason asks. He's too excited to modulate his tone. It carries across the room. One officer glances at us with a frown before turning his attention back to the camera screen.

"Shh."

"How do you know?" Mason asks in a lower tone.

"She saw him," Nat says. She gestures to the police officers. "You should tell them."

"What? No, I can't. They'll think I'm crazy."

Nat shrugs. "You're not crazy, but you have an ability that not everyone does. It will change how you live your life, so you may as well embrace it."

I can't do it. I slump against her knees, feeling as though I've let her down.

She smooths my hair. "It's a hard adjustment. I'll tell them this time, okay?"

I bite my lip, suddenly wanting to cry. I nod, knowing my voice will be hoarse with emotion.

"All right, everyone out," the officers shoo us off the stairs. "This is a crime scene now."

As we stand to leave, Nat says, "I think you'll find the body belongs to Jason Glinsmann."

"How do you know?" The younger officer shifts, his hand drifting to his holstered weapon.

His partner places a hand on his shoulder. "This is Natasha Patino. She's worked a case or two with us before. She's a psychic."

He relaxes incrementally. "So, you're saying you saw the ghost belonging to this skeleton?"

"Jason Glinsmann's spirit confirmed the bones were his." Her eyes meet mine and I nod, confirming she's telling the truth. I'm amazed she can be so honest about her abilities, but practically lie to the cops at the same time. Jason Glinsmann didn't tell *her* they were his bones. My palms are sweating just being in this situation. I hope they don't recognize me as a runaway, though what's the worst they can do? Tell my parents they saw me? I'm eighteen, old enough to leave home.

"We'll see what the lab says about that. Let's get out of the cellar. We'll take your information, then you can be on your way. No need to intrude on the Lees any more than we already have. We'll take the hatchet and knife with us, too. I don't know that there's any point, but I'm sure someone will enjoy analyzing them."

The police usher us out of the cellar. As we're leaving, I stop Mr. Lee. "Do you have a minute, sir?"

He nods and allows me to guide him to the side. I pull the necklace out of my pocket. "I found it in the attic. Nat says it belonged to a girl who worked here. She was probably a slave. It was precious to her."

He swallows, still staring at the small piece of silver. When he looks at me, his eyes are sincere. "I'll do my best to see if we can't find out more about it. Maybe find a living relative who would appreciate a family heirloom."

I nod, my eyes welling with tears, and place the necklace in his palm. "I really hope you find someone."

·········

After a shower at Nat's place, I sleep hard, waking to the long shadows of evening. Nat's spare room isn't glamorous—just a double bed and an empty dresser. It's not even very big, but it's warm and dry and mine. At least for a little while.

I grab my cracked—but fully charged—phone and pad out of the room in borrowed pajamas that smell earthy and floral at the same time. They smell exactly how I'd expect a psychic's clean laundry to smell. My own clothes are in the washer. I didn't have time to change the load before I passed out.

The living room is dim. A string of fairy lights hang on the wall behind the couch and candles are scattered around the room. The TV is on, the volume low. A nineties sitcom is playing, something I never got into. Nat is sitting on the couch beside another woman with long braids and glossy, dark skin. She smiles at me when I enter. Hesitantly, I smile in return.

"I just put on the kettle," Nat says. "Want some hot chocolate?"

I nod, unable to take my eyes off the stranger. "Who are you?"

I know my question is rude. This is Nat's apartment. But I was excited to spend time with her, learn her psychic techniques. Maybe she's Nat's friend, but the hand on Nat's thigh makes that seem unlikely.

Nat lifts the woman's hand to her lips and kisses the back of it. "This is my girlfriend, Autumn. Autumn, this is Lanie Gilbert. You two be nice, and I'll order some pizza."

I sink into the armchair next to the couch, pretending to watch TV, though my entire consciousness is on the woman a few feet away from me. I'll be here for a while at least. I need to like her. But I feel like she's intruding on the time I have with Nat. Or that I'm intruding on their time alone. I just want to feel like I belong somewhere. I'm tired of being the lonely outsider.

"Nat tells me you've got some abilities. What's that like? I've always wished I could do what she does."

"I don't know." I lean towards the TV. Nat is talking on the phone in the kitchen. I hear mention of pepperoni and bacon. Thankfully, no pineapple.

Autumn sinks back into the couch comfortably. Does she live here? That would be awkward for me. I sigh. Best to get used to it. I'm a guest, after all. I'm sure Nat will find some time to mentor me, even with Autumn around.

"Forty minutes," Nat calls from the kitchen. I hear a cupboard open and close, then the clink of a spoon against the inside of a mug.

Nat's phone rings while she's crossing the room with the mugs. She sets them down on the ottoman and fishes her phone out of her back pocket. "Hello?"

She retreats to the bedroom, so I can't hear the rest of the conversation, though I strain my ears trying. Autumn passes me a mug. I can't help but grin at her as the steam hits my nostrils. I sigh with satisfaction after the first sip. Sugar is really what I needed. This will all work out. I'll figure out my place.

Nat returns to the living room. "That was the police. They confirmed that it was Jason Glinsmann and wanted to thank us. They notified the family this afternoon."

"That's great," I say, half-heartedly. I bet his family never wanted to hear news of his death. If Jason was never confirmed dead, they could hope for his safe return. Tears well in my tired eyes. I don't want to cry, but I can't help but wonder if my parents feel the same way about me. I hope they do.

My phone chimes. I flip it over to see a text from Mason: *Mr. Lee just called to tell me you were right. It was the missing squatter. Good job. Want to catch up for coffee or something tomorrow?*

I ponder my response, before texting him back: *Sure.*

I keep it simply, worried he'll take my agreement the wrong way.

He quickly sends another text: *As friends only.*

My relief whooshes out of me in a long breath.

Nat gives me a strange look.

"You all, right?" she asks.

"Never better," I say with a grin. I actually mean it.

Epilogue

A couple of days later, Nat drives me to a diner on the edge of town. We take her car, not the motorcycle. Disappointing. Maybe she'll teach me to drive it sometime.

I've stopped here once before for a meal. It's a nice place. Fifties themed, complete with waitresses in poodle skirts, a jukebox, red booths, black and white tiles on the floor, and way too much chrome. Elvis's "Jailhouse Rock" is playing as I step inside. When I was here last, there were families and groups of friends at practically every table. It had made me realize how alone I was, sitting by myself at a table in the middle of the packed dining room. I hadn't come back because I didn't want to feel that way again. This time, as I step into the building, I'm not alone. Nat's here with me. And as we pause beside the sign that reads "Please wait to be seated", someone calls my name.

"Lanie, Nat!" Mason is standing next to a booth at the back, where Bethy and Conrad are already seated. "Over here."

I hold back the grin that threatens to split my face in half and make my way through the dining room. It's three in the afternoon, so the lunch crowd is gone and not many people are thinking of burgers for dinner yet. I had my shift at the Roasted Bean in the morning and this was the soonest I could make it.

"Hi, guys," I say, sliding into the U-shaped booth next to Bethy. Nat takes a seat on the other side, by Mason.

"You doing okay?" Bethy asks, pushing a menu towards me.

"I'm all right," I say. "My car should be fixed in a couple weeks. All it'll take then is a good cleaning."

"But she's agreed to stay with me for the time being," Nat interjects. It's been a bit of a hot topic lately. She insists I'm not intruding, but I feel like I am, and if my car is back in working order, I don't see why I shouldn't go back to living in it. Nat, and sometimes Autumn, argue that winter is on its way and I should stay with them until I'm able to find a place of my own. I've given in for now, but I can always change my mind.

"That's good. I don't think you should be sleeping in your car until they find that missing woman," Conrad says. He's been staring at his menu. I'd thought he wasn't listening.

I shrug. I still want my car. "Maybe."

"Hey, y'all," the waitress says as she approaches are table. "Ready to order?"

I nod. I already know what I want. "The beef hoagie."

It's the cheapest sandwich on the menu. I want heft to my meal, but I don't want to kill my paycheque with an expensive burger. The hoagie will still be delicious.

Once everyone has ordered, Bethy pulls out her laptop, and gives us a preview of the video from last Friday.

"We got so much evidence that I'm making it a two-part special. It's going to be great."

"Should we do a rundown of the spirits we think we encountered?" Mason asks. Before anyone can reply, he starts counting on his fingers. "There was Caroline and Lester, and—"

"Hold up, Mase," Conrad interjects. "Let's not worry about listing the ghosts by name. We have our thoughts on who we met, but we can't really be sure it was them."

"Says you!"

Conrad rolls his eyes.

"Nat." Mason turns to her. "Who do you think that dark presence you felt was? This house really seemed to affect you."

"Like Conrad said, it's difficult to say for sure, unless the spirit is forthcoming. But I'm inclined to say it was Lester, or Joseph Turner, the first owner of the place. That was his name, right?"

Mason checks the notes on his phone. "Yep."

"We talked to Lester, or at least I believe it was him. He didn't come across as violent at all in that conversation. I'm almost positive the dark presence was Joseph Turner."

I shift in my seat, uncomfortable. I don't want to ask this next question, but I need to. Riley saved me, and I need to know the truth. "Do you have a picture or something of Joseph Turner?"

"I do..." Mason scrolls through his phone. "There were none from when he was younger. I don't know how available photography was back then, but I do have one taken a couple years before he died."

He passes his phone to me. A grainy black and white photo of a man stares up at me. His pale hair is slicked back, but that beard is unmistakable, complete with tobacco stains around his mouth. His eyes are hard and mean, pale. They were probably blue, which doesn't match the black eyes of the spirit I saw, but it's him. One hundred percent, the ghost that attacked me was Joseph Turner.

"It's him," I say. "The evil presence tormenting the house is Joseph Turner."

"Really?" Bethy leans over my shoulder, peering at the screen. I let her take it, suddenly feeling nauseous. Riley saved me from this ghost. I haven't seen her since.

Nat reaches across the table, gripping my hand in hers. "We'll find her."

I nod, not quite believing her. What if Riley was defeated and went to wherever dead ghosts go? I don't want her to suffer, but I can't do anything for her until Nat and I find her. I blink back tears and paste a smile on my face. "You're right. We have to find her."

Our food arrives, giving me a welcome reprieve from my thoughts. I find I'm hungry despite my emotions, and I tear into my giant sandwich, polishing it off in record time. Nat watches me with wide eyes.

"I wish I had your metabolism," she says, taking a bite of lettuce from her salad. "Mine's nothing like it used to be."

"You're just old," Mason tells her. "One day, Lanie will be just like you. Ordering salad and drinking smoothies."

I grimace. "Thanks, Mase."

He grins at me, his eyes twinkling.

"What? You're being weird." I don't like his expression. It's foreboding.

"You called me Mase. That's the first time. You really do belong with us now, don't you?"

Heat rushes to my cheeks. I bow my head, shoveling my remaining fries into my mouth.

"Where should we investigate next?" Conrad asks. "Do we have any leads?"

I don't know if Conrad is trying to draw the attention away from me or not, but it works. Mason is immediately distracted.

"Nothing confirmed," he says. "But I've been hearing rumours about a restaurant here in town that's haunted. I'm hoping to convince the owner to let me investigate. I've called a few times, but he's always busy."

"What restaurant?" Nat asks.

"Janvier's. It's a fancy French place."

"Oof. Good luck. Do you know what they charge for meals there?" Nat sucks air through her teeth. "I doubt they'll want a bunch of ghost hunters running through the place, even when they're closed."

"It's worth a try." He waggles his eyebrows at us. "I've got a plan."

About the Author

Melissa Peters has always wanted to write. This first book is a realization that she can do more than dream-up stories—she can publish them too. She lives and works in Canada with her bestie and their four cats (yes, that's a lot). Creating stories is her passion; you can expect more from her in the near future.

If you'd like to stay up to date with her writing and get occasional news updates from her, check out her website and sign up for her newsletter. Her socials are linked there as well. She'd really appreciate if you took the time to review the book you just read. It would mean a lot.